Reunited With Danger

Reunited With Danger

Leann Anderson has spent the last fifteen years living far away and only coming home to visit. She's enjoyed her freedom but she misses her family. In town for her high school reunion, she thinks this just might be the right time to move back.

Zach Gibson thinks Leann is lovely and sweet, but as the little sister of his employer she's completely off limits. Look but do not under any circumstances touch. Per the bro-code, he'll simply have to admire her from afar.

So it's a surprise when Leann's brothers start to encourage Zach to spend time with her, pushing them together at every opportunity. Those Anderson men are up to something and Zach's determined to find out what it is.

But as the dead bodies of Leann's friends begin turning up at the reunion, Zach realizes they have a much bigger problem. There might be a serial killer on the loose in Tremont. And Leann just might be his next target...

Reunited With Danger

Danger Incorporated

Book Six

BY

OLIVIA JAYMES

www.OliviaJaymes.com

REUNITED WITH DANGER

Print Edition

Chapter One

IT HAD BEEN an evening of laughter, tears, and remembrance. Most of the women hadn't seen each other in years and they were anxious to catch up, sharing small anecdotes about their lives. Some of it was even the truth.

It had also been a night of celebration and the alcohol flowed freely. The usual inhibitions had dissolved away and the ladies ended up on the dance floor of the bar, whooping it up to musical memories and pretending they were teenagers again. For a few hours they forgot about mortgages, bills, and demanding families and instead let their hair down and became young and carefree.

But it couldn't last forever. Reality was heartless and one by one they left the bar to return to their everyday lives, whether good or bad. At least they'd have their memories to make them smile on those days when nothing seemed to go right.

Unlike some of the other women in the group, Carole Russell's life had turned out better than she'd ever hoped. She had a loving husband and two dogs of undetermined lineage that gave her unconditional adoration. She had a good job as a paralegal for a local real estate attorney and a beautiful home in a good neighborhood on the edge of town. Once a year, she and her husband took two weeks and went on travel adventures around the globe. Anyone looking at her would say she'd been lucky.

She doesn't deserve it.

After years of waiting, karma hadn't done its job. It was time to guide its hand.

Carole was one of the last of the group to leave the loud and rowdy bar, although there was still a half hour until closing time. She'd stopped drinking alcohol and switched to soda over an hour ago but it was easy to see that she was walking unsteadily, her body swaying as if a stiff breeze might knock her over.

That was the GHB that had been dropped in her drink when she wasn't looking. Carole had become disoriented and would probably pass out soon. She was in no shape to drive and her thought processes had become compromised with the drug. Her inhibitions were down.

In this, as in life, timing was everything.

"Hey, you look tired. Do you want a ride?"

Carole looked up from her purse where she had been searching for her keys. "That would be good. I stopped drinking awhile ago but I don't think I should drive. I feel a little woozy."

"I didn't drink so I'm good and sober. My car's parked behind the bar."

The two people walked out of the back door to the small, almost empty parking lot that was used mostly for the post office during the day. Most of the bar patrons used the front lot or parked on the street.

The front of the bar had cameras. The back, however, did not. It was an oversight that would surely be corrected after tonight.

"Let me get some of my junk off of the passenger seat so you can sit down. I'll just throw it in the back, give me a minute."

A hand wrapped around the tire iron sitting on the front seat, gripping tightly. Swinging around quickly, the metal bar came down on the side of Carole's head with a crunch. With a surprised cry the woman crumpled to the pavement, moaning as blood poured from the wound. Twice more the tire iron came down on her skull in rapid succession until there was a pool of red underneath the prone body. Two fingers placed on her pulse point told the story. Success.

Carole Russell was dead.

Chapter Two

IT WASN'T SUPPOSED to be like this. Leann Anderson had come home to Tremont for her fifteen year high school reunion to see a few old friends and catch up with her family. She'd made a few fleeting visits in the last couple of years but never anything that lasted more than three or four days. This time she was planning on staying two whole weeks.

She could end up staying even longer. For a long time now she'd missed her family terribly. It might just be time to move back to Tremont. She'd been making preliminary plans but that was a deep, dark secret she wasn't ready to share with anyone yet, least of all her family.

But she wasn't partying with her high school friends today. Her mother and father had met her at the airport this morning with horrible news. One of her classmates, Carole Russell, had been brutally bludgeoned to death outside The Tin Cup last night and a memorial service had been quickly thrown together by the reunion committee. That's why Leann was sitting on a metal folding chair in the Tremont Community Center. Bitty Glover, senior class president, was standing up at the podium crying and telling a story about her and Carole on prom night.

They'd drank too much spiked punch and ended up puking on their expensive dresses.

Moving back to a town with a killer on the loose didn't seem like the brightest idea but West, her brother and mayor of Tremont, had already pressed her oldest brother Jason into service. He ran a law enforcement consulting agency and cases like this were his specialty.

Sniffling, Bitty blew her nose and gave the somber crowd a watery smile. "I'll miss Carole more than I can ever express."

Leann and Carole had been friends back in the day, but not "best" friends. They'd socialized in the same circle and ended up at the same parties, even had crushes on the same boys. However, she wouldn't characterize herself as someone Carole confided her innermost secrets to. That had been Bitty. They'd been friends since kindergarten and their mothers were best friends as well.

"I know Carole would be overwhelmed to see so many of you here today. She was the kind of person who was friends with everyone." Bitty gestured to the long buffet table off to the side. "There's coffee, punch, and cookies. Please sign the large card on the table at the back for Carole's family. Also, we're taking up a collection to plant a tree in Tremont Park in her honor. Thank you for coming. The happy hour tonight at the hotel is still scheduled as are the rest of the events. I think Carole would have wanted the reunion to go on."

Everyone seemed to stand up at once, so Leann waited until her row had cleared out before making her way to the back of the room where Jason stood along with one of his employees. Zach Gibson. He was West's brother-in-law, which actually made him more than just an employee. He was family. In a way.

Tall, with light brown hair and shoulders as wide as a city bus, he was an imposing figure. Having met him at a few family get-togethers, Leann knew he was a black belt that had done a stint in the military before taking some personal security jobs for celebrities. Then he'd accepted a job with her brother Jason, and from what she was hearing was a model employee.

He was also gorgeous as hell and she turned into a stuttering teenage girl whenever she talked to him. It was sort of appropriate that he was here at her high school reunion. Her teenage self would have had a major crush on him.

But grownup Leann was going to act like an adult.

"Any leads on who did this?" she asked Jason and Zach quietly as her classmates milled around, chatting and drinking punch.

"No one saw or heard a thing," Jason replied grimly, a muscle ticking in his jaw. "The one thing her friends did say is that it seemed like she had drank far too much and was sweating and slurring her words."

"Is that how she ended up behind the bar when her car was in front?" Leann asked. "She got confused?"

Jason's brows raised. "I've got a theory about that. When we questioned the waitress, she said that Carole had switched to soda at some point in the evening. She should have been getting more sober, not less."

"And?" Leann prompted. "What does that mean?"

Crossing his arms over his chest, Jason sighed heavily. "Zach thinks Carole might have been dosed with a date rape drug. We've got the medical examiner looking for it in the tox-screen."

"That's awful. She might have been...assaulted before he killed her," Leann said, appalled at what she'd learned. "Do you think she fought back and that's why he...?"

Zach shook his head. "Doubtful if she was drugged. She wouldn't have been able to. In fact, she was probably doing well to stay conscious."

Jason patted her on the shoulder. "Hell of a thing to come home to. Are you okay, Sis?"

"Yes, I'm fine. Honestly, I don't think I've really processed it yet. I haven't seen Carole in years so it seems quite surreal." She took a deep breath. "Do you think this guy is going to strike again?"

"That's a question for Zach. He's become quite the profiler in the last year. I'm not sure whether to be happy or scared to death that he can get into these nut jobs' heads."

The man next to Jason shifted on his feet as his cheeks turned red. "I'll take that as a compliment. As for this killer, I'm not sure yet. I'm still questioning whether the murder was premeditated. Either way, this guy got a taste of killing last night and he might have liked it. There's also the open question as to whether Carole Russell was the intended target. If so, he may be done. He killed the person he wanted dead and that's that."

"I know I haven't talked to Carole in a long time but I can't imagine why anyone would want to hurt her," Leann replied, her mind running through images of the dead woman from the past. "She really was a nice person like Bitty said up there."

Zach's gaze went over her head to the crowd. "One thing I've learned over the years is that what a person allows you to see of their life is rarely the truth. Everyone has secrets. Even you and me."

That made Leann laugh. "My life is an open book. A boring one, so don't read it when you're sleepy."

Rubbing his chin, Jason cleared his throat. "So about this case… Leann, I need you to do me a big favor. It would really help out the investigation."

Anything she could do to help, she would. He ought to know that but he was acting like he was about to ask for pint of blood or her firstborn child.

"Whatever you need, big brother. I'd love to be able to be of some assistance, although I'm not sure what I can do."

"I'm glad to hear you say that." Jason shot a glance over his shoulder and then took her arm, leading her into a small alcove with Zach on her heels. "Listen, are you still planning to attend the reunion events this week?"

"I am. That's why I came home."

"Do you have a date?"

"No," she answered carefully, watching Jason's expression. What was her brother up to? Did he want to tag along?

Jason smiled triumphantly. "You do now. I need you to take Zach to the events so he can observe and mingle with the reunion guests. One of our theories is that the killer is one of your former classmates."

Startled by her brother's request, her gaze flitted to where Zach was leaning against the wall, a patient look on his face. Apparently he wasn't as sure about this plan as Jason was, which was kind of a letdown. It wouldn't be a hardship to take him, although it wouldn't quell the attraction she felt for him but that was her problem. Perhaps if she spent more time with him she'd find out he picked his teeth and belched after meals. The old familiarity breeds contempt argument.

It was just that…

"No one is going to believe that we're dating," she pointed out. "I've been gone and he's been here."

"We've thought about that," Jason replied. "If anyone asks, tell them that you met him at the wedding and that he's traveled to visit you a few times. He's gone on business quite a bit so it's a good cover story. Will you do it?"

She couldn't say no. This was a murder investigation, for heaven's sake. There wasn't one good reason not to and she did want to help. She turned her attention to Zach who so far hadn't said much, but then he didn't talk much around her.

"You know that you're going to be bored stiff listening to stories about people you've never met before?"

Zach nodded. "That's the plan. I'm looking for someone who might have had a beef against Carole Russell and decided to use the reunion to get some revenge. You won't even know I'm around. You don't have to babysit me. I can take care of myself."

Leann would definitely know he was around. He was too big and muscular to ignore. She wouldn't want to meet him alone in a dark alley and he had a sinister vibe that kept people at arm's length.

Zach *looked* like a mean dude that could kick some ass. Intimidating as hell.

"Okay," she capitulated with a sigh. "But I want to apologize up front about all the crazy stories you are going to hear. And if you hear one about me? It's all a lie. Lies, lies, lies. Don't believe a word anyone says. I was an angel back in high school."

As far as her family knew.

✦ ✦ ✦

ZACH WOULD BET his next paycheck that those stories about Leann were the truth. A cute little redhead like her probably had a million guys chasing after her in high school, plus just as many friends to party with. Her teenage years, unlike his own, had been happy and carefree. Her biggest worry was what she was going to wear to the big game or maybe whether her latest crush liked her back. He'd been busy simply surviving, for himself and his two younger sisters.

Jason nodded toward Leann where she was chatting with a few friends. "You're okay with this, right? Leann's a good girl and she's easy to get along with. She'll be able to answer any questions you have about her classmates."

"I'm fine with it as long as she's okay with me tagging along."

"She doesn't mind," Jason assured him. "Believe me, she would have said something if she did. She's very direct. She doesn't play those mind games that other women do. You can count on her to tell you the truth."

Okay, that was a weird statement from Leann's brother. Why would Zach need to know she wasn't like other women? This was an assignment, not a date.

Zach was well aware of the bro-code. A guy didn't express romantic interest in a friend's little sister. Period. He might think Leann was beautiful and sweet and just the kind of girl he'd like to get to know better, but he wasn't about to ask her on a date. A real one. She was off limits and in a way, it made things easier. After all, there was no point in getting involved with a female that wasn't going to stay in Tremont. Leann would be gone in a few weeks and Zach would still be here. He'd grown to love this little town.

"What's your gut saying about our theory?" Zach asked as he studied the interactions between people. This was his favorite part – reading their body language and facial expressions. "Do you think this murder has to do with the reunion?"

Grimacing, Jason shrugged. "If you want a true gut check, you have to talk to Logan. He's the one with the almost perfect instincts. But I do think the timing isn't coincidental. Carole lives in town and the killer could have done this at any time but he chose last night. What are you thinking?"

"I'm not ready to say what I'm actually thinking. Not yet, anyway. I do think we need to go through the usual suspects. Statistically the most dangerous person in a woman's life is her husband or boyfriend."

"We talked to him," Jason pointed out. "He seems to be genuinely tore up about her death."

"Just in case we should have Jared check out the family finances. Look for any insurance policies or large debt. I don't think he did it but I want to rule him out early if we can. I'm also going to talk to her coworkers this afternoon. Maybe they might know a few of Carole's secrets."

Jason chuckled and shook his head. "On the contrary, you are going nowhere. Logan is already at her workplace questioning her friends and boss. You are staying here with Leann. You're her date for these festivities, remember? Your assignment starts now."

Zach's second surprise of the day. He hadn't realized just how serious Jason was about mingling with this group of former classmates. If this is where his employer wanted him to be then that's what he'd do. He spotted Leann across the room, talking to three other females. Time to make his presence known and get to know some of these reunion-goers. One of them might be a cold-blooded killer.

Chapter Three

LEANN'S BEST FRIEND Desiree "Dizzy" Foster looked up from the book she was reading and tossed it aside with a groan. "You're going to wear a hole in my floors the way you're pacing over there. Since when are you nervous about attending a barbecue? You're acting like this is your first date."

Pausing in the middle of the living room, Leann gave her a withering look. "You'd be nervous too if you thought that one of your classmates was a killer. Add in the fact that I'll be going with Zach and this evening becomes a tad more difficult than it should be. Why did I say yes to Jason?"

The evening was going to be awkward as hell. She barely knew Zach and now she was supposed to pretend they were boyfriend and girlfriend. Subterfuge was not her strong suit. They'd managed at the memorial service earlier in the day, although it had felt strange for him to be so close and follow her around as she visited with her old friends. It hadn't helped that she thought he was attractive too.

"Because it was the right thing to do," Dizzy answered promptly. "I've only met him a few times but Zach seems like a nice man. You'll have a good time and he'll do his job. It's all good as long as the rain stays away. And the killer too, of course."

"Is it supposed to rain?" Leann groaned, peeking out the front window to see if her escort had arrived.

"It's supposed to but maybe it will hold off. Did the reunion committee get a tent or one of the pavilions in case of bad weather?"

"Pavilion three. It's near the lake."

"Do you really think that one of the reunion attendees did that awful thing to Carole?" Dizzy asked, her teeth sinking into her bottom lip. "It's scary to think that there is a killer running loose around Tremont. I always think of this town as boring as hell."

"It usually is, but I guess like every little town it has its moments. As to whether I believe it, I don't know. The timing could be a complete coincidence. I'll leave the sleuthing to Jason and Zach." She slumped against the window frame. "Maybe it was a mistake to come back. This could be a sign that I'm supposed to stay in Florida."

Rolling her eyes, Dizzy laughed. "Since when do you believe in signs? Besides, I don't like hearing you talk like that. I want my best friend back in Tremont. Have you said anything to your family yet?"

Double hell no.

"I have not and I expect you to keep the secret as well. You're the only one I've told that I'm thinking of moving back. They're upset enough that I'm staying with you in town instead of staying out at the ranch. I don't need to compound that by dropping a bombshell that I'm maybe coming home but I'm not sure. They'll lose their minds and attack me with all the reasons I should leave Florida, and they're not above using guilt to get their way. Jason told me today at the service that Mom was looking thin and sick these days. You know, like she could keel over any moment because I don't live here."

Dizzy held up her hands in surrender. "I won't say a word. Scout's honor."

"You were never a scout. Your mother said that clubs that wore matching outfits only create sheep that blindly follow the government."

Louis and Tamera Foster, Dizzy's parents, were as unique and eccentric as their daughter. Now retired, they were currently spending the summer in Greece volunteering at an archeological dig.

Dizzy's smile grew wider. "I wanted to be a Girl Scout so badly but Tami put her foot down. She hated conformity. Did I tell you they called this morning? They're having a blast. They might get invited to work on another dig in Canada when this one is done."

"I'm happy for them. They worked hard and they deserve to enjoy their retirement but you must miss them."

"I see my parents a lot more than you see yours."

Dropping the curtain as Zach pulled his SUV into the driveway, Leann retrieved her purse and checked her lipstick.

"I see what you did there," she said, shaking a finger at her friend who only laughed in return. "I do miss them but they also make me crazy. My parents aren't like yours. They weren't out there encouraging me to experience life and be free from society's expectations. Mine were the opposite and being an Anderson has an entire set of rules all its own."

Dizzy picked up the book she'd discarded earlier. "Screw the rules. That's what I always do."

Words to live by, but it wasn't always easy. Leann didn't have time to ponder her friend's advice because the doorbell was ringing. Zach had arrived and it was time to introduce him to all of her high school classmates.

The females were going to love him.

✦ ✦ ✦

LEANN INTRODUCED ZACH to all her old friends and the females gushed and flirted as if their significant others weren't standing less than a foot away. Sexy in a strong and silent sort of way, his sheer size commanded attention wherever he went. He was easily six-three or four with a muscular build that made him look fine indeed in the faded pair of denims he wore that molded to his powerful thighs. The navy blue t-shirt he wore showed off his perfect flat abs and just a smidgen of a tat on his left arm. It was all she could do not to reach over and lift his sleeve to take a closer look.

Look but don't touch. That's not what he's here for.

"Leann, I heard you were in town!"

Jenna Marshall, Leann's best friend from the age of ten practically ran across the room. They'd been through everything together from braces to boyfriends, although they'd lost touch in the years since graduation. Life always got in the way. Jenna looked amazing, but then she always did. Blonde and blue-eyed, she was the quintessential girl next door and everything Leann had wanted to be back in their high school days.

"Here I am," Leann laughed, giving her friend a hug. "I was hoping I'd see you today. I missed you at the service yesterday."

Jenna's smile fell. "We couldn't make it, unfortunately. One of the kids had a fever but I made a donation for the tree. I still can't believe she's gone."

That last part was delivered in a whisper.

"Neither can I. I keep thinking I'm going to see her alive and well, smiling like always." Remembering that she had a companion at her side, Leann stepped back to introduce Zach. "Jenna, this is Zach Gibson. Zach, this is Jenna Marshall. She and I were best friends back in high school."

Jenna laughed and shook Zach's hand. "I could tell you some stories about this girl. You're Gigi and Aubrey's brother, right? You work for Jason?"

"I am and I do," Zach agreed. "Best job I've ever had."

"Are you working on this case? Do you know who did this awful thing?"

Zach's expression turned sober. "We don't yet but we will. We're determined to bring this person to justice, ma'am. That I promise you."

Leann looked over Jenna's shoulder. "Where's Drew?"

"That's a good question. I bet he's wherever the kegs of beer are. All he's been talking about for a week is hanging out with his old football buddies." Jenna linked her arm with Leann's. "I'll introduce you, Zach, but I warn you he'll probably press you into service on his softball team."

"I wouldn't mind that," Zach laughed.

They walked out of the pavilion and toward the bonfire but didn't make it three feet. Blocking their path was Troy Wallace, wide receiver on the football team and the guy affectionately known all those years ago as "Jenna's stalker". He'd had a crush on her since grade school from what Leann had been able to tell. Adulthood didn't appear to have cooled his ardor at all if the look on his face was anything to go by. Of course, Drew had his own admiration society from high school and Nicole Quincy had been the president.

I wonder if she's here tonight?

Leann actually felt a little sorry for Troy as he stood there, his eyes alight with happiness. Time had been kind to Troy, though. He was still in good shape and had all of his hair. The only tell-tale sign that he'd already had too much to drink was the high color in his cheeks. He must have started early.

"Hey Jenna, you look beautiful."

Troy was standing a little too close and Jenna took a step backward to put some distance between them, but gave him a dazzling smile in welcome. She was nothing if not polite. "Thanks, Troy. You remember Leann Anderson, don't you? She's back in town from Florida for the reunion. And this is her date, Zach Gibson. He's fairly new in town but he works for Jason Anderson."

Surprisingly, Troy was able to tear his gaze from Jenna to greet Leann and Zach. "Of course, Leann Anderson. Your last name is plastered all over town. That's hard to forget. How are you?" He shook hands with Zach. "Nice to meet you."

Inwardly she winced at his statement but knew it was true. It was one of the reasons she'd left Tremont. She was never referred to as Leann but always as Leann Anderson…of "those" Andersons. She hadn't done anything to earn the fame; her family had done it for her.

"Fine, thank you. It's nice to see you again."

"Yeah." So much for reconnecting with old classmates. Troy's attention was firmly back on the blonde at her side. "So…Jenna…save me a dance tomorrow night?"

Jenna's gaze slid to the bar area on the right side of the room. "I'm not sure what Drew has planned. Can I get back to you?"

Brows pinched together, Troy gave a growl in reply. "Do you need Drew's permission? Is he that much of an asshole? He hasn't changed."

Easy there. That escalated quickly.

Beside her, Zach immediately tensed as if for battle so she placed her hand on his arm to calm him. Troy was harmless. Annoying but basically a pacifist. He wouldn't be starting any fights tonight. Not sober, anyway.

Stiffening, Leann's friend crossed her arms over her chest and huffed. "My husband is not an asshole. I just don't know what the plan is for tonight, but if you're going to act like this then the answer is no. Shove off, Troy. Let's make it another fifteen years before seeing each other again."

Another growl but Troy stomped away, a scowl on his face and Jenna heaved a sigh of relief. "What a jerk. He hasn't changed a bit."

"No, he hasn't," Leann agreed, letting Jenna lead them toward the bonfire area. "If anything, he's become even more angry than he was back then when all he wanted was to bask in the gloriousness of you."

Jenna waggled her eyebrows. "I am glorious, aren't I? I need to be worshiped more."

"I'll talk to Drew and the kids about that."

"Good luck," Jenna pouted playfully. "They don't appreciate me."

Leann nodded to where Troy was talking with some old buddies from the team. "He does."

Rolling her eyes, Jenna shook her head. "I'll pass. Maybe I'll come back as a goddess in another life. The goddess of cooking and cleaning."

"People always love a good cook."

Zach was giving Troy some serious side-eye. "If he bothers you again, Jenna, please let me know. We have deputies patrolling the event and I can have him escorted off the premises."

Jenna waved away his concern. "That's so sweet but Troy is all talk. He'll stay away as long as Drew's around."

Speaking of Drew… Jenna's handsome former quarterback husband was sitting at a picnic table full of friends and Leann could almost remember all of their names. Cindy. Trent. Marianne. Bill. Henry. She wouldn't relive her teenage years for all the money in the world.

Funny how being back in Tremont with all of her old friends seemed to make the intervening years dissolve away to nothingness. She had to make a concerted effort not to let anyone or anything wipe away all the progress she'd made these last fifteen years. She was more than her last name.

Two hours later after chatting and catching up with old friends, Leann needed a break. Luckily Zach found a quiet spot on the edge of the party where she could get a few moments of peace and quiet. Balancing her paper plate filled with a cheeseburger and potato chips on her lap, she carefully set her soda can on the ground next to her lawn chair. Zach had surprised her by being prepared and bringing two of those collapsible chairs that folded up into a bag and she was damn grateful to have a place to sit down.

"I don't think I have this straight," he said, popping a chip into his mouth. "Bitty and Carole were best friends and you and Jenna were best friends, but you traveled in the same clique."

"It wasn't a clique, it was just a group of friends. This isn't *West Side Story*."

The cheeseburger was juicy and delicious and Leann hummed in appreciation. It had been too long since lunch. Zach was enjoying it as well if the big bite he'd just taken was any indication.

"A group of friends is a clique," he pointed out. "I assume you were in the popular crowd at school?"

Stiffening, she wasn't sure if she liked his tone. He made it sound like a bad thing to be liked. "I don't know your definition of popular. If you're asking if I had a lot of friends, well, then I guess I did. There was a group of us that ran around together."

He put down his burger and their gazes clashed. "Which one of your friends was Homecoming Queen? Or was it you?"

Shifting uncomfortably under his gaze, she cleared her throat. "It was Jenna."

"Hmmm…that's what I mean by popular but you already knew that, didn't you? It's funny how you want to pretend that you were a geek or an outcast of some type when you clearly were part of the privileged few at your school."

She definitely didn't like his tone. "Now wait a minute, I wasn't some sort of princess. I worked hard and got good grades.

I'm not sure when that became a bad thing. I wasn't some sort of *mean girl* if that's what you think. I got along with everyone."

She wasn't sure why his opinion of her was so important. She barely knew Zach.

"You certainly were luckier than many of your classmates."

Zach was treading on dangerous territory and he needed to back the fuck up. He didn't know what he was talking about.

"I am aware that I was born into a wonderful family but like everything else in this life it comes with its own set of responsibilities. It isn't all tea parties and cotillions, for your information. I lived my life in a fishbowl, always being watched. It can get on your nerves after awhile and I was just a young girl. I didn't always handle it well."

He looked like he wanted to say something but instead he changed the subject back to her friends. "Let's talk about the people you hung out with in high school. Were any of them mean girls? Did they bully some of the other kids?"

His blue gaze saw way too much without her even having to say a word out loud.

"Sometimes but it was mostly the boys giving wedgies or stuff like that. Girls were more...passive aggressive. They just wouldn't invite someone to a party or to go shopping. That's how females do it. They ostracize."

Stretching out his long legs, he took the last bite of his burger. "And who was the ring leader? Who decided who got in and who didn't?"

"This is why I hate revisiting the past," she muttered and sighed. "I think everyone had their moments when they were being a bitch."

"There's always a leader of the pack, though. Who was it?"

"Carole," she found herself answering, her thoughts shifting back to fifteen years ago. "Carole had a strong personality even then. She was a natural leader."

"But Bitty was senior class president. How did that work out?"

It was so long ago. "Carole was ill and wasn't able to start our senior year until about a month into the school year. Is it important?"

"Probably not," Zach dismissed it easily. "It's just an interesting dynamic and it's my job to try to understand everything that's going on here. All the relationships, whether good or bad. What about Troy Wallace? What's his deal?"

"He's always had a thing for Jenna and she's never returned the feelings. End of story."

"Did Carole turn him down as well?"

That's where Zach was going with this? He thought Troy was a suspect?

"Not that I remember."

There was a low rumble of thunder and a flash of lightning. Storms rolled in quickly around here and before she knew it the sky had turned black and rain was coming down, soaking her, Zach, and the remnants of their dinner. He grabbed her by the hand and they ran up to the pavilion to get shelter from the deluge along with all the other guests.

Cramped into the small space with a hundred other people, she was pressed against Zach's solid body as they listened to the storm rage. He smelled…good and he felt…better. She shouldn't be enjoying this as much as she was. This wasn't a real date. Besides, she had the distinct feeling he didn't like her much. At the very least, he didn't approve of her.

Not that she cared. She was going to be more like Dizzy. To hell with the rules, full speed ahead.

Chapter Four

ALL THE REUNION guests had gathered under the protection of the pavilion, huddled close together not because they were cold but because there were too many people shoved into a small space. Luckily, the storm passed quickly and the crowd began to move back into the open again. A couple of guys grabbed a bat and ball and started a pick up softball game out in the wet field.

Leann was chatting with her friend Jenna, but she excused herself and joined Zach as he watched the game. "We don't have to stay if you're bored. I don't mind leaving."

She sounded like she wanted to go but didn't want to admit it was her idea. Had she had enough of nostalgia for one evening?

"I'm fine. We can stay as long as you like."

They sat quietly for a half inning before she spoke again. "It looks like they could use someone like you in the game. I think most of these guys don't get out and exercise much."

What they lacked in skill, the men made up in enthusiasm. They were having a ball, although it might have more to do with the amount of beer imbibed than the physical exertion and competition.

"Someone like me? I'm not sure I follow."

He didn't even like baseball all that much, and he couldn't remember the last time he'd played it. High school, maybe?

"You know…you're in shape. I bet you play lots of sports."

"You'd lose that bet," he laughed, keeping his eyes on the game. "I'm not a big team sport kind of guy. I'm more of an individual competitor. For fitness, I do mixed martial arts. I have since I was in the Army. It's a great workout, plus you learn to handle yourself in a fight."

"I took a self-defense class in Florida. It was interesting."

"Interesting? I would hope it would be more than that. Do you feel confident that you could take on an attacker?"

Her lips twisted and he had his answer. "Sadly, no. I walked out feeling confident but I think if those skills aren't practiced a lot they tend to fade away. If confronted I'd probably panic and scream."

He made a mental note to mention this to Jason. Hopefully as her big brother he could convince her to take another class or six. Even in a small town like Tremont it was better safe than sorry.

"Never underestimate the power of a good, loud scream at the top of your lungs. It's saved more people than you'd think. Criminals don't like their victims to call attention to themselves."

As if on cue, a blood-curdling scream ripped through the air, getting everyone's attention. The softball game stopped and everyone stood still until the second scream sounded. A woman ran out of the brush around the lake, waving her arms and yelling.

Not hesitating, Zach took off toward her, running right through the game and capturing the female by the shoulders so she had to look up at him.

"Ma'am, are you okay? What's wrong?"

Face pale and eyes wide, she waved an arm toward the lake. "It's Bitty. Larry and I were walking along the bank and then we saw her. She was just lying there with her eyes open, kind of staring at us. Oh God, Bitty's dead."

Jesus, not again. Right out here in the open too. The killer was brazen to do something like that. He was gaining confidence. They could have been seen by anyone.

Bitty and Carole were friends and possibly rivals as well. Now they were both dead. There had to be a connection.

But the more pressing question? How did Leann fit into all of this? These were women from her group of friends. Was this revenge of some kind against the popular girls in high school? As far as Zach was concerned that put Leann right into the crosshairs of a killer.

✦ ✦ ✦

ZACH KNELT DOWN next to Bitty's body, Jason hovering over his shoulder.

"From the marks on her neck I'd say she was strangled, maybe with a rope of some kind. Her clothes are also soaked so I'd put time of death during the rainstorm that came through here. I'm guessing the killer lured her away from the group and then used the thunder and rain as cover for what he was doing."

"Then it ought to be simple," Jason observed. "Who was

missing during the storm?"

"That's not an easy answer. We were all stuffed into that pavilion like sardines. We can ask Leann but I'm not sure she'll even know. Her classmates brought husbands and wives with them, people she wouldn't recognize."

Straightening, Zach moved away from the body to let the newly arrived medical examiner do his job. There was a line of people, including Leann, being held back by a few deputies. Everyone wanted the one thing Zach didn't have. Details. Like the murder before, they were scarce.

"Let's step over here so we can talk without anyone overhearing us," Zach suggested, leading Jason to an area by some trees.

"Do you know something?"

Zach's gaze ran over the crowd of reunion guests, looking for…what? Someone that didn't fit in? Or looked guilty? Perhaps someone that didn't look horrified?

"Whoever this is isn't dumb," he said. "He did this in the rain, washing away a lot of evidence. He also didn't use his bare hands to strangle her. That might have left prints we could use. Whatever he did strangle her with he had the sense to take with him as well. But this does have one thing in common with Carole Russell's murder. It looks like these women trusted the killer. There aren't signs of much of a struggle or defensive wounds. Bitty walked out here with her murderer as if he was a close friend."

A muscle ticked in Jason's jaw. "No witnesses, too. Why do I have a feeling this guy is just getting started?"

"I've got the same feeling. He's become bolder and more aggressive. All of the girls in Carole and Bitty's social group need to be on their guard. The buddy system at all times."

Jason's head shot up and his eyes narrowed. "Leann was their friend. They all hung out together."

Zach had already thought about that but he took no pleasure in bringing this subject up to his employer. "If someone is here at the reunion looking for revenge, anyone in that social circle needs to be careful. That includes Leann. We may be way off here about the killer's motivation but I'm just going with what we know."

"I hope you're wrong," Jason replied grimly. "But in case you're not, your number one priority just changed. You need to keep my sister safe no matter what. You stick to her like glue. I'll get Logan and my family to help out. Until we find this guy I don't want Leann to be alone."

Zach had known this was coming. Nobody could close ranks like the Anderson family.

"I won't let anything happen to your sister but we have another issue. How are we going to everyone safe? Should we ask the committee to call off the reunion?"

"I thought about that but what if he simply raises stakes and leaves? Then we'll never get him. Both of these women lived in Tremont so the killer could have gotten to them at any time if he lived here. I think he's from out of town."

Maybe. Zach was leaning a different way.

"Or he could have waited until the reunion because of its symbolic nature. Bringing everyone together from his past and making a big show of the killings. Look at how he leaves the bodies where they can be found easily. He wants people to know what he's done because he's proud of it. It could be his way of saying 'How do you like me now?' That means he could be from here. So far he's certainly known his way around. He knew that the back of the bar didn't have cameras and he knew about the lake."

Jason cast a glance over his shoulder at the crowd watching their every move. "I don't like this at all. I'm going to talk to West and the chief of police about putting extra patrols around the reunion dance tomorrow night plus a few plainclothes cops inside the event. In the meantime, we need to go warn the reunion guests. A few left after Carole's murder and I'm guessing a few more will after this."

"I'm surprised you're not trying to talk Leann into going back to Florida."

Barking with laughter, Jason shook his head. "Have you met my little sister? She's as contrary as they come. When we want her to come home, she won't. I bet if we told her to leave, she wouldn't do it. Frankly, I think the safest place for her is here where her family can watch over her. I wouldn't sleep well at night if we just sent her back without a second thought. We don't know what lengths this killer is willing to go to and I don't want to find out by getting a call from the Florida cops that Leann is dead."

Zach understood wanting to protect family. He'd do anything to ensure Gigi and Aubrey's safety. Besides, today hadn't been so bad. He'd enjoyed talking to Leann and spending time with her. West and Travis had protected his sisters when he couldn't be there. It was time to return the favor.

He would keep her safe and alive from a killer who might not be finished.

✦ ✦ ✦

ZACH'S FINGERS DRUMMED against the steering wheel as he drove Leann home. They'd barely said a word since leaving the park and that had been fine with her. After what had happened, she wasn't sure what she was supposed to say or feel. She only knew that she was horrified by Bitty's murder.

Who was doing this? Who had enough hate and resentment in their hearts to kill the two women?

"Your brother is worried about you, Leann."

Zach's voice pulled her from her dark thoughts but it gave her something to concentrate on other than the image of Bitty lying on the grass beside the lake.

"I know," she replied, swallowing hard. "He thinks that someone wants my social circle dead, doesn't he?"

"It's one theory, based on the current evidence. Do you have another one?"

No, she didn't, although she wished differently.

"I'm not the cop here, you are. What do you think?"

"I think you need to be very careful going forward." There was a long pause. "Your brother asked me to take the lead in protecting you. Not let you out of my sight and all that. I agreed, of course, but no one has talked to you about that. Are you okay with it being me? If not, I'm sure Jason can ask someone else to do it."

It was thoughtful…asking for permission. Something her brothers had never heard of in their lifetimes. She often wondered how their wives put up with their alpha male, high-handed bullshit. If she didn't let Zach, then one of her brothers or cousins was going to do it and then she'd be behind bars for murder.

"It's just fine. I'll try not to be a problem or anything."

"Just try?" he chuckled. "Are you normally difficult to be around? I think I should know ahead of time what I'm getting into."

Shrugging, she tried to craft a diplomatic response. Oh, what the hell. He was family so he might as well know where the skeletons were buried.

"If you ask my family – the male ones, anyway – they'll tell you that I'm stubborn and bossy. That I don't take suggestions well and that I'm obstinate for no good reason."

"What would the female ones say?"

"The few females that we have in the Anderson family would say that I grew up with so much testosterone in the house that I was practically drowning in it. I had to learn to fight back and stand my ground early or I would have been run over by a bunch of boys who thought they knew what was best for me."

He didn't answer right away, absorbing her answer. "Is that why you moved out of Tremont? Because your brothers tried to run your life?"

That was the easy answer but it was more than that. "That was part of it but it was really that I needed an identity separate from being an Anderson. I love my family, Zach, but growing up I was known as the *Anderson girl*. I just wanted to be Leann."

He pulled up in front of Dizzy's house and put the vehicle in park. "Did it work?"

She nodded. "It did but it's lonely too. I miss my family and friends. I miss living in a little town like Tremont. But I'm glad that I moved away. It helped me grow up and stand on my own two feet. I'm not sure I would have learned how to do that when my brothers were determined I wasn't going to make any mistakes. Sometimes that's the only way to learn."

"Do you think you'd ever move back?"

That was the million dollar question.

"It's possible. I don't have anything to prove anymore."

"I think your family would be glad to have you back, especially now that your brothers are having kids of their own."

As close as Zach was to Jason, she couldn't take the chance and admit to him just how close she was to returning.

"I've given it some thought." Pushing open the car door, she turned back to bid him goodnight. "Thank you for driving me home and being my escort. I guess I'll see you tomorrow night for the dance?"

Zach's smile grew wider as if something was amusing him. "Maybe I wasn't clear earlier in the conversation. I'm your new bodyguard, Leann. You go nowhere without me or someone else that Jason has assigned. Now head inside and pack a bag. You're coming home with me where I'll know you're safe."

Hold the phone. What? Home. With Zach.

Leann hadn't seen this coming at all.

Chapter Five

LEANN HAD ARGUED with Zach but that had been a complete waste of her breath. Even Dizzy had agreed that Leann should take every precaution for her safety. Dizzy wasn't worried for herself as she wasn't in the same class as Leann, nor had she been in the same social circles. Zach had offered to stay at Dizzy's and sleep on the couch so Leann wouldn't have to pack up, but his large frame on the tiny sofa would be an engineering feat. No way was he going to fit, let alone comfortably.

So she packed her things and followed him without complaint. Well, not too much.

Since moving to Tremont he'd purchased a small bungalow in a family-oriented neighborhood not far from Jason and his wife Brinley. Unlike many bachelor pads she'd seen, Zach's house was decorated and homey with photographs framed on the mantle and walls, big throw pillows on the sofa and in front of the fireplace, and the scent of… Was that potpourri, or maybe a candle?

"This is nice," she remarked as he set her suitcase down at the entrance to the hallway. "You've certainly done a lot to the place. Is that cinnamon I smell?"

Shrugging off his light jacket, he hung it on the peg next to the door before taking hers and doing the same. "I made snickerdoodles last night when I couldn't sleep. There are dozens left. Are you hungry?"

Snickerdoodles? The huge muscle man with a black belt made cookies? Hell yes, she wanted one. Maybe more.

"They sound yummy. They're one of my favorites." She followed him into the kitchen. "Do you bake a lot?"

She wanted to ask him even more questions but she didn't know quite how to phrase them. The house looked like a *home.* Like a family lived there, not a single guy who traveled all the time.

Then a horrible thought occurred to Leann. What if he had a girlfriend he lived with and she had done all this cozy decorating? What would she think about him bringing home a stray that he had to protect from a killer?

After washing his hands he placed cookies on two plates, handing one to her. "As much as I can. I had to learn to cook and clean when I was younger and taking care of Gigi and Aubrey. Of course, back then gourmet cooking was macaroni and cheese. I hope I've improved a little bit since then."

She bit into the chewy cookie and the flavors exploded on her tongue. Damn, this was good. "I think you've got a lock on this cookie recipe. These are delicious."

He pushed the cookie jar closer to her. It was a bear with a big stomach and the head came off so a person could reach in to get the cookies. "You can have as many as you like. If you're hungry for real food I can fix you something. I try and keep my pantry well-stocked."

Him or this woman she hadn't seen yet?

Looking around casually, Leann popped a second cookie into her mouth. "So do you…live here alone?"

She'd tried to make the question sound natural but Zach wasn't fooled. He smiled and laughed a little, his own gaze roaming his comfortable home.

"I do and I know what you're thinking. Others have commented on it, too. It looks like a woman lives here."

She didn't want him to think– Shit, she didn't know what she wanted him to think.

"No, that's not what I was asking at all."

He dug three more cookies out the jar. "I don't mind explaining. When me, Gigi, and Aubrey were growing up we didn't have anything like what you would call a home. We lived in a cramped, run-down apartment because that's all my mom could afford. She had a bad drinking problem and there was never enough money. All of our furniture, clothes…everything we had really was someone else's castoffs. We ate cheap food and prayed that we didn't get evicted, which by the way happened quite a lot. So I always told myself that when I had the chance I would have a real home. It may not be the most masculine thing to pick out color swatches and dishes but I don't care. I have what I've always wanted."

Tears stung the backs of Leann's eyes. She'd heard about his childhood but she hadn't connected that to this. Zach was clearly nesting here and building the life he hadn't had growing up.

"I…I don't know what to say. I think it's lovely but I can't help but feel badly about your childhood years. You must think

I'm the most spoiled woman on the planet to complain about my family growing up when you had to deal with much more than I could ever imagine."

His gaze fell to the floor and she realized she'd hit the nail on the head. He had thought she was a spoiled rich girl. But then he looked up and their gazes clashed, his own blue eyes dark with emotion.

"I did kind of think that until I actually met you. It's just that your family would go on and on about how they missed you. From where I was standing it seemed like you didn't care. Of course, I should have known it's never that simple. It's just…I would have given anything to have a family like yours."

This man was so surprising. He looked big and tough, rarely speaking. But when he did he had a raw honesty that touched her heart. With his childhood he should have been hiding his emotions, scared to trust but he was just the opposite. He simply put himself out there and the world could like him or not.

"You have them now," she replied softly. "And thank you for not hating me. I swear I'm a nice person."

"I know that. I'm sorry for thinking that you weren't, even if it was for a short time. It couldn't have been easy growing up with the name Anderson."

Her problems were petty compared to his. "You can't even compare it to your situation. It's so superficial."

He braced his hands on the counter and leaned closer. She caught a whiff of his scent, clean and manly. Just like him. "It's not a contest, Leann. Which one of us had the worse upbringing? My problems don't make yours any less real."

"I think about it, you know," Leann found herself saying.

His honesty pushed her to be more as well. "Moving home."

"Your family will be thrilled if you decide to." He held up his hands in surrender. "But don't worry. Your secret is safe with me. I have a feeling if Jason knew you were thinking about it you'd never hear the end of it."

"You know my brother well," she joked, grabbing another cookie. "I appreciate your discretion. You know, your house is better decorated than mine is. I feel like a home economics failure. These cookies are better than mine too. If you can make lasagna I'm going to crawl away in shame."

Luckily, he took her ribbing well and threw his head back and laughed, rich and warm. My oh my, Zach Gibson was an attractive man. The fact that he could color coordinate a kitchen and make cookies only made him more so.

And I'll be living here until the killer is caught.

"If it makes you feel any better Aubrey helped a little. She has a good eye for color so she'd show me paint and fabrics and I'd say yes or no. But the cookie recipe is all mine." His eyes twinkled as he smiled. "And I make a mean lasagna. A good pot roast too."

"Will you share your recipes?"

Rubbing his chin, Zach appeared to think about her question. "I'll make you a deal. If you let me show you some self-defense moves, I'll share my recipes. Deal?"

With a killer on the loose, it wasn't a bad idea to learn more about defending herself. Plus, these cookies were fantastic.

"Deal."

Maybe staying with Zach wouldn't be so bad after all.

✦ ✦ ✦

ZACH WASN'T A good sleeper at the best of times but when he was trying to keep another human being safe it was even worse. Jason had sent him a text that the cops were going to send regular patrols by the house and Zach had an excellent security system, but he still couldn't rest comfortably knowing that there was a killer out there going after popular girls from Leann's class.

Was it revenge? Or was someone using the reunion as a cover for something else? A sleight of hand to push the investigation in one direction while the guilty party pursued their real target? There simply wasn't enough evidence at this point to decide.

Knowing he wouldn't sleep much tonight, he made a saucepan of hot cocoa – a better version than the one he'd made for Gigi and Aubrey all those years ago – and camped out in front of his laptop to do some research on the two victims. It was possible the women had more in common than just being friends all those years ago. He was deep into Carole Russell's financials when he heard soft footsteps behind him. Leann.

"Couldn't sleep?" he asked, twisting in his chair to where she was standing at the entrance of his kitchen looking positively adorable. She was wearing red plaid flannel pajama pants and an oversized grey sweatshirt. Her feet were bare and she'd polished her toes a bright scarlet that should have clashed with her hair, but somehow didn't.

She's off limits. Don't forget.

"I thought I was being quiet. How did you hear me?"

"Too many nights on patrol in the Middle East. Would you like some cocoa? The warm milk will help you sleep."

He didn't wait for her to answer, simply standing and pouring a mug of the lukewarm concoction. The microwave would have it steaming hot in no time.

"I woke up and couldn't get back to sleep," she explained, sliding into the chair opposite him. "What's your story?"

Chuckling, he handed Leann her cocoa and sat down again. "I've never been a good sleeper. As a kid I always had one ear cocked for trouble and I guess it's a habit now."

Her expression sobered and he wished he hadn't mentioned his childhood again. She was a soft touch, clearly. "That must have been so hard on you…to be the man of the house at such a young age."

Smiling, he shook his head. "I don't feel sorry for myself, Leann. My upbringing kind of sucked but it made me who I am today. That and a decade with Uncle Sam. It's all good, I promise. I don't think of myself as a victim of society or anything like that. There are lots of people in this world that have it much worse than I did. I had my sisters and that made all the difference."

Tucking her feet under her, she sipped at the hot liquid. "You're very well adjusted. People could take a lesson from you."

"Perspective is a gift and combat is happy to give it to you," he chuckled, remembering his years in the military. "Bad things happen to everyone. It's how you deal with them that makes the difference."

Leann gazed down at her mug as if it held the secrets to the universe. "Is that what this is? My turn to have something bad happen?"

"The cynical in me might say yes, but my gut tells me that

what's happening here as very little to do with you and everything to do with the killer. These are his issues, not karma pulling up in front of your house." But that brought up another question. "Are you saying that nothing bad has ever happened to you?"

Pursing her lips, she considered his question. "Nothing too terrible or out of the ordinary. I lost my grandparents and that was sad. I've buried a few family pets and I still get teary-eyed about them. I had a friend who was sleeping with my college boyfriend behind my back. Does that count?"

"Yes, it does and by the way, she obviously wasn't a friend if she did that. Are you worried that because you haven't had life smack you between the eyes that something really bad is going to happen? Like there's a rotten luck quota and you haven't been dealt your cards yet?"

The sheepish look she gave him answered his query. "I feel like I'm sitting here waiting for the other shoe to drop. Like perhaps my life has simply been too happy and the shit is about to hit the fan."

"There's nothing wrong with having a happy life, Leann."

Propping her chin on her hands, she frowned at his statement. "But you said that what you went through built character. What if I lack character?"

She was truly worried about this but she didn't need to be. But it said a great deal about her that she was. Most people wouldn't give it a second thought.

"I said it made me who I am. I'd like to think that I already had some character to begin with. Adversity simply taught me perseverance, not integrity. You have character."

"I know I've been lucky," she finally said, the words simple but almost apologetic. She didn't need to be sorry about that.

"I'm glad that you have. I don't go around wishing that people had lousy childhoods. That would denote a serious lack of character, don't you think?"

He'd finally managed to get a smile from her. "I guess you're right. You could have been a psychologist."

"It's fascinates me but I don't have the patience to listen to people tell me their troubles day in and day out. I'll leave that to you. You're the shrink."

"I couldn't do what you do either. Being in charge of someone's security is a big deal."

He couldn't help but laugh at the horror in her expression. "It's all about protocols and following them. Which reminds me, I have to go to the office in the morning so Jason is going to send out one of the other guys to hang out with you until I'm back."

"Do they know the protocols?" she teased, her hands wrapped around the mug. "Can't I just go with you?"

Good question. Why not? The safest place for her would be at the office.

"If you like, but I can guarantee you it will be boring as hell. I have to do a little bit of paperwork. It won't take long, though. We can go out to lunch or something if you like. Then maybe a self-defense lesson."

She nodded and then pointed to his laptop. "So what did I interrupt?"

"I was just looking over some information about the two victims. Their friends, family, careers, finances. Anything and everything that might give us a clue as to why they were targeted."

"Any luck?"

"Not yet, but I still have quite a bit to go through."

She peered around to see the screen of the computer. "I could help. I doubt I'm going back to sleep any time soon."

Zach could use the help…

"Are you sure? It's like looking for a needle in a haystack."

"You tell me what to look for and I'll do it."

That was the thing; he didn't always know. "Anything that doesn't look normal. Debt. Arrests. Family or marital issues. It could be anything."

"How would you know they were having marital issues?"

He turned his laptop so she could see the document he had pulled up. "For example, they might have credit card charges to a doctor or therapist. Or maybe the husband spent a lot of money on hotels, jewelry, and lingerie. Maybe the wife recently bought a gun or talked to an attorney. Perhaps the husband made regular cash withdrawals but the amount is too large to be pocket money. Small actions can have big consequences."

Leann's eyes had lit up and she looked eager to help. "I can do that. It sounds fascinating."

"Tell me that when you're almost cross-eyed in a few hours. Just let me dig out my tablet and you can work on that, then I'll make us some more hot chocolate. Should I get the cookie jar too?"

Zach could get used to this. Having someone to share a long, dark night with. Someone who was interested in his work. He chuckled inwardly that she found it fascinating. It wasn't but it was sweet that she was all gung-ho about it.

But before he settled in he gave himself another stern reminder. Leann was off limits. Way out of bounds. And even if she wasn't, she wouldn't be here in Tremont for long.

Chapter Six

STEPHEN GLOVER WAS a good looking, blond-haired man in this early thirties who was currently wearing a determined expression. He'd been waiting by the door of the consulting company offices when Zach and Leann had pulled up this morning. Now Zach had Stephen sitting in their one and only conference room with a cup of coffee and one of the glazed donuts that Jason had brought in while Leann set up in her brother's office.

"Do you want me in there with you?" Jason asked. "I can be, if you like."

"Give me ten or fifteen with him," Zach replied. "Then come join us. I'm guessing by then I'll have a better idea of why he's here. You can visit with your sister while I'm talking to him."

Chuckling, Jason refilled his coffee. "Then I'll give you twenty. I can definitely use the time to catch up with Leann. Brinley was bugging me last night about having her over for dinner, which means you would come too, of course. While you're in there I'm going to check what Jared dug up on the Glover family. Maybe there will be something we can talk to him about."

Joining the bereaved husband, Zach sat across from him and took a sip from his coffee cup, still sizing up the situation. This was highly unusual, a family member showing up here at the offices. Normally, Zach questioned them in their own home where they were comfortable. If they were a suspect, he might question them at the police station.

He decided to keep the conversation friendly and neutral. Let Stephen drive until Zach figured out why he was here.

"How can I help you, Mr. Glover?"

The man's eyes were red-rimmed as if he'd been crying most of the night. He looked worn out and ready to sleep for a week.

"I want to know what you're doing to find the man that killed my wife. I can't get any answers at the police station. They said that your firm had taken over the investigation."

Zach nodded. "We have been asked to consult on the case as we have extensive experience with murder investigations. As for what we're doing, I can assure you that we're doing all we can to find the person who did this."

Stephen glanced down at the coffee cup sitting on the table in front of Zach. "I don't see you doing anything so far."

Glover thought the cops were sitting around sucking down java and watching Netflix?

"I can assure you that we're on top of this. Any physical evidence has been sent to the state crime lab and we have to wait our turn for results. As for questioning any persons of interest, that task is split between the police and our firm." Time to turn the tables on Stephen. "Since you're here, would you mind answering a few questions? It would be extremely helpful to the investigation."

Zach had questioned the husband briefly last night at the barbecue but the man had been so overwrought it was difficult for him to concentrate. Better luck might be had today. He didn't wait for Stephen to give permission.

"How long had you and your wife been married?"

Glover was just tired enough not to have the energy to object. "Almost ten years. We met in college and got married after I finished law school. We moved here about five years ago to be closer to her mother. She's not doing so well these days."

"So you didn't know many of the people at the park last night?"

Stephen shook his head, a haunted look in his eyes. "Just the ones that I've met in Tremont these last couple of years. I never thought–"

He broke off, choking as a sob made it difficult to speak. Zach changed the direction of the questioning from last night.

"Does Bitty have any enemies in town? Someone with a grudge?"

"Everyone liked her," Stephen replied, a note of desperation in his voice. "She volunteered at our kids' school, she worked part-time at the craft shop and gave scrapbooking classes. She taught Sunday school at our church. Bitty was a wonderful woman. Why would someone do something like this?"

A straightforward question with a murkier answer. "The reasons people do what they do aren't always clear. He could be angry with Bitty or she could represent someone else, someone that he wants to hurt. At this point I can't tell you which it is." He paused before plunging forward. "Did Bitty ever talk about her high school days?"

"Some. She liked high school and she had good friends."

"So she was popular?"

Shifting in his chair, Stephen appeared confused. "I guess you could say that. What does that have to do with anything?"

Zach wasn't ready to answer anyone else's questions. He still had a few of his own.

"Did Bitty ever turn down a guy for a date and make him mad? Did she have any admirers that didn't take no for an answer?"

Glover's eyes widened. "Do you think…? This could have been some guy who never got over his crush. Jesus, what's the world coming to?"

From what Zach had seen? Hell and a hand basket.

"Did she mention anyone?" Zach pressed. "Anyone at all?"

"No, she didn't." A rush of tears fell from the husband's eyes, dampening his cheeks. "Bitty didn't deserve this."

"I know and we're going to do everything we can to bring the killer to justice." The door swung open and Jason strode into the room, file folder in hand. "Mr. Glover, this is Jason Anderson, the head of our consulting firm. Jason, this is Stephen Glover."

The two men exchanged a handshake as Jason sat down next to Zach. Jason opened the folder and shuffled through the contents, letting Zach know silently that something had come up in the background check. It was typical to go through a murder victim's life and finances with a fine-tooth comb.

"I just have a few questions, Mr. Glover. Stephen. Is it okay if I call you Stephen?"

"Sure." Glover shrugged awkwardly, glancing back and forth between Zach and Jason. "What do you need to know?"

"Do you have any enemies, Mr. Glover? Anyone that might want to hurt you by hurting your wife?"

"No, I told your colleague here." He pointed to Zach. "There's no one."

Jason pulled a piece of paper from the file and pushed it across the desk to Glover. "Can you explain this for me?"

Rubbing the back of his neck, Stephen gave the paper a cursory glance. "This isn't what it looks like."

Jason sat back in his chair. "Then what is it?"

"Yes, my brother and I got into it about six months ago when Bitty and I were visiting my folks in Seattle. A few punches were thrown and the neighbors called the cops, but it was simply a family disagreement."

"What was the disagreement about?" Zach queried.

"Leland wanted to borrow money…again. He has trouble holding down a job because he drinks too much. Bitty and I knew he would probably ask again when we were in Seattle and we'd decided to cut him off. He got angry and physical and I defended myself. End of story."

Stephen shoved the paper back at Jason, who took it and placed it back into the folder.

"Does he still have a drinking problem?"

Glover squirmed in the chair, his gaze darting around the room. "We've tried to get him help but so far it hasn't worked."

Jason glanced at Zach, nodding. "The murderer here in Tremont is highly organized, Mr. Glover. He makes plans and sticks to them. He's detail oriented and he's patient. It doesn't sound like your brother fits that profile. Thank you for answering our questions. I know how distasteful they can be but we do ask them for a reason. We can officially rule him out now."

Stephen Glover didn't seem relieved at that bit of news. If anything, he was more angry.

"I could have told you he didn't do it. Why aren't you out there looking for who did this?"

Jason stood, tucking the folder under his arm. "We are looking, but you have to understand that we must rule out the family members first. Statistically speaking, people are generally not killed by strangers. They're usually killed by family and friends. That's why we have to do this. I know it feels like an invasion of privacy–"

"You can't possibly know how this feels."

"But this is how we find the murderer," Jason went on as if Stephen had never interrupted. "We rule people out one by one until we have a small pool of suspects to closely investigate. I apologize for upsetting you after all that you've been through. Unfortunately, this is my job and sometimes it can rub people the wrong way."

Jason left the room, leaving Zach with a fuming Stephen Glover.

"So what else are you doing to do to find this guy?" the husband finally asked. "Can I expect more embarrassing questions about my friends and family?"

"It's possible," Zach conceded. "If we find something in our research we may have to ask you about it. We are sorry but being polite isn't going to catch this guy."

Glover seemed to digest that statement before answering.

Leaning forward, he tapped the table with his index finger.

"Then ask me anything you fucking want because I want this guy caught and put behind bars for the rest of his life. Just do that and I won't care what you say to me."

"Believe me, that's what I want too. I'm going to find him and justice will be served."

With any luck, before the killer had a chance to strike again.

Chapter Seven

THAT AFTERNOON, LEANN was beginning to regret her deal with Zach regarding self-defense lessons. He'd dressed in a pair of sweat pants and a tank top, and she was reminded of just how...big...he was. He was like an oak tree, tall and solid and she was the opposite. She trusted him not to hurt her during the session but she wasn't the most graceful person on the planet. She might simply injure herself being a klutz.

A big smile on his handsome face, Zach rubbed his hands together excitedly. "Are you ready?"

This so-called lesson was being carried out in the middle of a deserted martial arts gym where apparently Zach was a good friend of the owners, because they'd told him to "lock up" when he was done.

"I guess so. Am I dressed okay for this?"

At home Leann walked on a treadmill and sometimes played tennis so she wasn't sure what the proper attire was for getting her ass kicked. She'd chosen stretchy shorts and a t-shirt. No tennis shoes allowed on the mats, so she was also barefoot. The germaphobe in her shuddered at the thought but Zach didn't seem bothered in the least so it was probably fine.

His grin widened and he motioned to her t-shirt. "It's fine. I like your shirt, by the way."

It was plain gray cotton with a bright pink rabbit wearing work out gear, and it was one of her favorites. Every time she wore it someone commented on it.

"Thanks, I thought you might get a kick out of it. Get it? A kick?"

Perhaps she could distract him with humor and he'd forget they were here for self-defense classes.

He was holding his stomach and laughing. "Got it. That's cute. I may have to get one just like it."

In a much bigger size.

"I might want to mention now that I'm a little nervous about this," she said before he could continue. "I'm kind of clumsy."

"It will be fine," Zach assured her. "Let's start by warming up some, get your muscles ready to work. I don't want you to be too sore tomorrow."

"I am definitely going to be sore if we do more than a brisk walk. You might say I've been neglecting my workouts lately."

Zach nodded as if he understood, which clearly he didn't by the looks of him. "Work making it tough to get to the gym? I know how that goes."

"No, you don't," she answered promptly with an eye roll. "Look at you. You're in incredible shape. You're probably one of those annoying humans that get up when it's dark outside so they can exercise before going in to work. As a mental health professional, I worry about people like that."

"I've been in better shape, believe it or not. But once you get in shape it's easier to stay there."

"It's the getting there that's the tough part," she said knowingly. "I've tried before but I have trouble sticking to a workout plan."

"Then it wasn't the right workout for you. You need to find something you enjoy."

Leann enjoyed binge-watching bad television shows while eating a pint of Ben and Jerry's. Sadly, she hadn't managed to burn one calorie doing that yet.

"That's what in shape people always say but it's bull. Sweating isn't pleasant."

Chuckling, he walked over to the corner of the room and retrieved two jump ropes.

"Then you're going to be very unhappy in about an hour. Let's jump rope for a few minutes to get the blood pumping."

She could do this. Many happy recesses had been spent with her friends jumping rope. It was like riding a bike and she was eight years old again.

Except that she didn't remember huffing and puffing this much when she was in third grade. She hadn't had breasts either back then and having them bounce up and down was uncomfortable. After about a minute, she had to take a break to suck oxygen into her lungs while he jumped easily, not even breaking a sweat. Smooth bastard.

The rest of the hour didn't get any easier. Zach had her gouging at his eyes, punching his solar plexus, stomping on his instep, and her favorite – kneeing him in the balls.

"Now what do you do when I raise my hands to defend my eyes?" he asked as she struggled to catch her breath. There was no doubt she was going to be sore tomorrow. And the next day too.

"Knee you," she replied, supporting her torso with her hands on her knees. "Then plot a most painful death."

Bending so he could see her face, he flipped her long braid over her shoulder. "Had enough for one day? We can practice again another time."

Crumpling to the mat, she stretched out and closed her eyes, pillowing her head on her hands. Now this was comfortable. "Just wake me up when it's time to go to the dance. No, better yet, wake me up when it's time to catch my flight back to Florida."

She thought she heard him step away so she was surprised when she felt a few cold, wet drops on her forehead, but damn it felt good. Her lids fluttered open and he was kneeling next to her on the mat, a water bottle in one hand with droplets sliding down the sides.

"Time to rehydrate. You need to drink it all."

She didn't argue, twisting off the cap and drinking down half of it at once before falling back to the mat. "Pure ambrosia."

Zach sat crisscross, his own water bottle empty and tossed aside. "Are you really okay? Do I need to carry you out of here? I don't want to have to tell Jason that I broke his sister."

Giggling at the thought of that conversation, she rolled to a sitting position. "I doubt he'd be surprised."

"Weren't you a cheerleader?"

She drank down more of her water. "I was young and limber and I looked cute in the outfit. Don't judge."

His grin was wicked and evil. "I'll just bet you did. Did you wear a short skirt and jump around?"

Her cheeks were red and it didn't have anything to do with physical exertion. "Maybe. Is it important that I did?"

"Just trying to get a picture here. Are there any photos?"

"Yes, and Mom will probably entertain you with several picture albums at Sunday dinner if you ask. But I beg you…don't ask."

Rubbing his chin, he had a devious expression on his face. "I'll tell you what. You do a little cheer for me now and I won't ask your mom for photographic evidence."

"More deals? What is it with you?"

"I believe in win-win."

She just bet he did.

"I think I remember one but I'm going to need a little something more. If I show you a cheer, you have to show me some of your martial arts. Maybe it will inspire me to get a black belt or something."

It wouldn't at all but he didn't know that.

"That's a deal I'll take all day long. I'll even go first so you can rest up a little bit."

Already warmed up, Zach didn't waste any time. He moved through what looked like a choreographed set of kicks and punches, rather graceful for a man his size. When he was done, he bowed and then plopped back on the mat with a grin.

"Your turn."

"That was really, really good. You must have studied for a long time to be able to do all of that."

He hopped back up to his feet and reached his hand down to help her up. "Years. Your turn."

Leann wasn't going to be able wriggle out of this one by flattering him. Dammit.

Standing straight and tall with her arms at her sides and her heart racing, she closed her eyes and thought back to all the words and moves from those days so long ago on the sidelines. The sounds of the crowd and the smell of the grass and sweat. Her family and friends in the stands cheering her on. Slowly it came back to her, her body stepping through the routine with increasing confidence, even the jump at the end. She was sure she looked ridiculous but in a million years she'd have never believed she would even remember it, let alone do it.

When she opened her eyes Zach was grinning like a loon. "You were incredible. My God, woman, you are just amazing."

Somehow she must have thrown herself into his arms in triumph because their faces were so close…and their lips… She could drown in his soft blue gaze as their mouths drew ever closer to one another.

His warm mouth had barely brushed hers, setting off a cacophony of sensations inside of her when his phone went off, the loud ringer piercing the quiet. Jerking away, he took several steps back, his shoulders rising and falling rapidly with his breathing.

"I need to get that."

Numbly she nodded, telling herself that it could be something about the murders. She might have believed it too if Zach hadn't looked so relieved about the interruption.

He'd simply been caught up in the moment, and that hurt more than the workout did.

Chapter Eight

THE CHEESY PURPLE and gold banner hung over the entrance to the hotel ballroom, trumpeting the event that Leann Anderson had been dreading for weeks. All the pre-reunion activities had been leading up to this night.

Tremont High School Class of 2002 Reunion.

"Are you ready to do this?" Zach asked, straightening his tie. He cleaned up nicely from his usual casual slacks and jeans. Tonight he was wearing a dark blue suit that looked like it had been made just for him, molding his wide shoulders and tapering to his lean waist. Zach was a handsome man by anyone's standards. A man that wasn't for her. He'd made himself clear that afternoon at the gym.

Stop staring at the man, Leann. He doesn't want you.

Still, it wasn't his fault that he wasn't into her. He hadn't asked for this assignment. After her earlier humiliation, she'd vowed that tonight she would be friendly and casual. He'd never know that she'd been hurt by his rejection.

"Does it matter? We have to do this. We have two murders to solve."

"No, I have murders to solve. You have a reunion to attend.

You need to stay out of the investigation. If anything happened to you, your brothers would beat me senseless."

"Are you afraid of my brothers?"

Chuckling, Zach grinned at her question. "Singly, no. But when they gang up on a person? Fuck, yes."

The table by the entrance was covered with name tags and Leann found hers but almost pretended she didn't. It had a grainy black and white photo from her senior year in high school. It was hard to believe but yearbook pictures could actually look worse.

Like when they were pinned to Leann's cleavage.

Zach's gaze lingered on her chest. Maybe he didn't dislike her after all. He appeared to like what he was seeing without being a creep about it. "Nice…picture."

Way to send me mixed signals.

"It's horrific and you know it. My only comfort is that most everyone's photo is going to be this bad." Leann's nerves ratcheted up a notch as her gaze darted around the room. "Now what's the plan? Do I need to steer you to certain people or are we going to mingle casually?"

"Let's start mingling casually and if I see someone I want to talk I'll either say something directly or nudge you in that direction. Deal?"

"Sounds fine." She nodded to the smiling woman heading straight for them. "That's Jenna Marshall. You might remember her from last night."

For the dozenth time, Leann had second thoughts about even being at this reunion. If she hadn't promised Jason to bring Zach she probably would have skipped the entire party tonight.

She'd remembered why she hadn't spoken to most of these people in fifteen years.

She didn't like them much. They probably didn't like her either.

Visiting the past was a stupid thing to do but here she was – rubbing elbows with people she'd rather not see again. Most of them, anyway. She was happy to see Jenna, despite not keeping in touch as well as she could have. Leann hated electronic communication, preferring face to face.

Pretty blonde Jenna looked especially lovely tonight. "There you two are. I've been looking for you everywhere. We have a table near the bar. Come join us. Everyone is having a great time and there's champagne." Hugging Leann, she gave Zach a flirty smile. "Just try not to drink too much tonight like you did graduation night. Remember how you ended up puking all over the back of Drew's truck?"

Why yes, Leann did and she was so happy that Jenna had brought that moment up right in front of Zach.

Why do I care what he thinks?

Because you do. You like him even if he doesn't like you.

"I could do without memories like that."

Jenna just laughed. "Remembering the stupid things we did is half the fun. Now smile and show all the people here how great your life turned out and how fabulous you look. Lots of people are going to want to see you tonight. Now, let me take a look at you."

With all the people milling about in the entryway of the hotel ballroom this was hardly the ideal spot, but Leann knew from experience that Jenna was like a dog with a bone when she got an idea in her head. Better to give in on the small stuff and then dig her heels in on something bigger.

Obediently taking two steps back, Leann looked down at the black silk slip dress she was wearing. She'd spent way too much time picking it out but she was happy with how she looked in it. The dress was held up with spaghetti straps that highlighted her year-round Florida tan and showed a hell of a lot of leg, ending at mid-thigh. Silver sandals with a four-inch heel gave her more height than her usual five-foot-five.

"You look gorgeous," Jenna pronounced with a big smile. "Doesn't she look beautiful, Zach?"

Leann wanted to dig a hole and crawl away, but Jenna and everyone else thought that Leann and Zach were a real couple.

"She does, indeed. You both do," he replied gallantly. "Now which way are we going, ladies?"

Straight to the bar. Chattering and giggling, Jenna led them to a long table filled with Leann's former classmates. There were several open bottles of champagne on the table and it looked like they'd been drinking for awhile.

Henry Chambers, a guy who had sat behind her in geometry, stood up with a grin on his face.

"Is that Leann? Wow, you look great. Come sit by me."

Oh fuck no. The way Henry was swaying on his feet told her he'd had at least one too many, probably more. And hadn't he married at some point? Was his wife here or was he divorced?

Zach's arm tightened around her waist. "Sorry, Leann's with me. Sweetheart, can I get you a drink?"

She needed to remember to thank him later. Henry had always given her a strange vibe and it wasn't a pleasant one.

"Dirty martini and make it a double, please."

Leann had a feeling it wouldn't be her last drink tonight.

✦ ✦ ✦

THE BALLROOM WAS a crush of bodies, the largest crowd yet at any of the reunion functions. After mingling for awhile, Zach found himself on the dance floor with Leann. It was a good way to get a good view of all of the guests without looking like he was watching them. He wasn't flush with rhythm but he had a few moves that kept him from being totally lame. Leann, on the other hand was fantastic, her body movements graceful. He didn't want to enjoy being this close to her but he couldn't help himself. She was an attractive woman and his love life pretty much sucked because all he did was work.

He'd almost kissed her at the gym this afternoon and he was equal parts relieved and regretful. He did desperately want to kiss her but he was having trouble reminding himself that she was off-limits. Jason would geld him with a dull spoon if Zach touched his little sister. Thank God his phone had rang because he hadn't been about to stop. Her lips had been far too tempting.

Trying not to think about how her body brushed against his and how his pulse raced whenever she was in the room, Zach asked her question after question about the people in attendance. Anything to get his mind out of the gutter and back onto the case. He couldn't seem to drag his gaze away from the curtain of fiery red hair, the mouthwatering curves shown off to perfection in that black dress, and most of all that creamy skin that begged to be touched and caressed. Every time she twirled, her skirt lifted and revealed a tempting amount of thigh that almost had him on his knees in worship. It was only through hard won self-control and the memory of his employer that kept him from pulling her a little closer or maybe trying to steal a kiss in the shadows.

Jesus, it's like the surface of the sun in here.

He'd worked up a sweat and he could use something cool. "How about I get us a couple of drinks?"

"That sounds like a great idea. Just a soda for me. I'll see if I can get us a table."

Her reply was drowned out by the sounds of angry, raised voices near the men's room. At three inches over six feet, Zach had an excellent vantage point to see what was going on, and from where he stood it looked like Drew Marshall and Troy Wallace were in each other's face. Troy was shoving his finger into Drew's chest – an aggressive move – and Drew wasn't backing down. Even from here Zach could see their faces, bright red with fury. If they didn't cool down right away the altercation was going to deteriorate into a brawl.

Leann stood on her tiptoes, her gaze darting around the room. "What's going on? I can't see a thing."

"Drew Marshall and Troy Wallace are going all caveman on each other. Wait here."

Now this was interesting and just might be the break he needed. Zach thrust himself headfirst into the crowd that had gathered around the men. Shouldering his way through the crush of bodies, he managed to insert himself between Drew and Troy just as the latter threw the first punch. Zach awkwardly caught it and he had to brace his legs and spread his arms out, placing a hand on each man's straining chest.

"Just fucking stop it. If you want to beat the hell out of each other, take it outside."

Where I'll follow you to see what you're arguing about.

Troy pointed his finger toward Drew. "I'll take it outside if he has the guts. I don't think he does."

Pushing against Zach's hand, Drew replied with some trash talk. "I'll meet you anywhere at anytime and kick your ass."

"Big man with this guy protecting you," Troy jeered, spittle flying out of his mouth.

Zach wanted to punch both of these guys. Just because. He hated it when men put their testosterone on display in some childish effort to one-up the other person. This was behavior that should have been left in high school.

"He's protecting you, asshole," Drew growled.

Sick and tired of their juvenile bickering, Zach gave each of them a big shove backward. "I'm not protecting anyone but the innocent bystanders."

Jenna Marshall ran up to Drew clearly distressed with tears in her eyes, tugging at his arm trying to pull him away from Troy. "Just stop it. Stop this right now. He isn't worth it. You'll end up spending the night in jail."

Troy tried to push closer but Zach held him back. "I didn't do anything."

Jenna looked over her shoulder at the other man, her lips pressed into a thin line. "Shut up and get out of here, Troy. I don't want you. No one wants you."

Was this over Jenna?

Drew rubbed his chin and then seemed to relax. "You're

right, babe. You're right."

She caressed his cheek and he leaned down to give her a brief kiss before returning his attention to Troy.

"Stay the fuck away from my wife."

Troy grinned and laughed. "Or what?"

"Or you'll regret it," Drew said quietly, anger still written clearly in his features. "Come on, babe. Let's get back to our friends."

Drew and Jenna disappeared into the crowd that was quickly dispersing now that the excitement was done. Troy, however, didn't seem ready for it to be over and he kept throwing his arms in the air and running off at the mouth about how everyone always took Drew's side.

Leann joined Zach, handing him a tall glass of water. "I thought you might want something cold to drink. That certainly was interesting. Are you okay?"

He rubbed his right shoulder where Troy's fist had glanced off of him. "I'm fine. Troy doesn't have much of a right hook. I think Drew could have taken him."

Crossing her arms over her chest, she watched as Troy headed out of the main entrance to the ballroom. "He's had a crush on Jenna for years but I've never seen him go after Drew. At least, I've never witnessed it."

A guy with a temper like that didn't suddenly acquire it. Zach would bet his next paycheck that wasn't out of character behavior for Troy Wallace.

"I think he had too much to drink tonight and let his old crush get the better of him. Hopefully he'll be embarrassed tomorrow morning."

Leann gave him a dubious look. “Maybe. He was mumbling and complaining under his breath as he walked out of here. That’s not the action of a sorry man.”

“I said he’d be sorry *tomorrow*.”

“I stand corrected.”

He drained the glass and set it on a side table. “I think I told you to stay put.”

She nodded, mischief in her brown eyes. “I have poor listening skills. I also don’t work well with others or share my toys. Back in first grade I brought in candy but not enough for everyone in the class.”

“I just wanted to keep you safe but clearly you’re a menace to Tremont society,” Zach teased. They were having a great time together. It was almost like a real date. But not quite, of course. Because she wasn’t for him and he fucking needed to remember that. “Now how about that drink?”

Jenna bounded up to them, smiling now that the situation was resolved. It appeared that Troy had left the reunion so all was well in the world. “Zach, Leann, come join us, you two. We’re going to do a toast to the Class of 2002.”

Jenna had quickly retreated back to her table and friends but the invitation was still open. Zach raised an inquiring brow to Leann. It was up to her.

“So would you like to join your friends?”

Better to be in with a group of people than be alone with her. His mind was going places that he knew better than to visit.

“I love champagne,” she said with a smile, linking her arm with his. “What about you?”

He hated the stuff but it was the beverage of the evening, so he'd deal with it. It was, however, a much-needed reminder that they'd lived very different lives. He was a kid from the streets and she'd been born with a silver spoon.

"Lead the way."

Chapter Nine

"I CAN'T BELIEVE all these geeks that grew into doctors and lawyers," Darrell Madison said as they all sat at the table drinking champagne and listening to Sheryl Crow. "I guess I should have studied harder in high school but I was too busy getting laid. You know what? I think I had the better end of the deal."

Leann winced at Darrell's crude words. The star forward on the basketball team had never been known for his sensitivity but apparently his manners hadn't become any better in the last fifteen years. The beer and champagne he'd pounded probably didn't help the situation. Darrell was putting away some serious amounts of alcohol and that was only what she'd seen since they'd joined the group for the toast. His face was bright red and his movements were clumsy. Zach must think she went to high school with a bunch of drunks.

Darrell apparently wasn't done making things even more awkward. "Who are you, man? Did we go to school together? Did you play defense?"

Inwardly Leann groaned at her former classmate and wished she sat closer so she could kick his shin under the table. As if sensing her unease, Zach patted her hand under the tablecloth. "No, I didn't go to Tremont High but I am Leann's escort for the evening. I work as a law enforcement consultant for Jason Anderson."

Zach was being nicer than Darrell deserved.

"Word around town is that you were in the military over in the Middle East and then you did personal security work for a few celebrities. Any stories you can tell about the rich and famous?" Jenna asked, playing the peacemaker as usual.

"Not in mixed company."

Everyone laughed and seemed to leave the topic behind, content to talk about the people who hadn't shown up, wondering what had happened to them.

"Leann? Leann Anderson?" A familiar man stood just behind Zach and Leann, his face wreathed in smiles. "Jesus, I can't believe it's you. You look fantastic. Do you remember me? Colin Simpson."

Colin. He was the reason she'd passed chemistry and physics.

Grinning, Leann pushed back her chair back and gave the other man a hug. "I had no idea you were going to be here. It's so wonderful to see you. Colin, I don't think you know Zach. He's new in Tremont. Zach, this is Colin Simpson. He helped me with my science homework so I could get into a decent college."

Zach smiled and shook the other man's hand. "Good to meet you."

"Nice to meet you, too. Tremont is a great little town." He turned his attention back to Leann. "I was hoping you'd be here. I think the last time I saw you was right after graduation. I know you moved out of Tremont. What have you been doing?"

Leann pointed to the empty chair across from her. "Join us and we can all catch up."

Darrell snickered at his end of the table. "More geeks. I think it's a conspiracy."

The average IQ of the table just went way up when Colin sat down.

Colin nodded toward the far end of the table. "Darrell Madison, right? No one could forget you or your infamous fart games. They were legendary."

Darrell elbowed Drew. "See? He appreciates my sense of humor."

Drew shook his head and took a swallow of his beer. "He's being polite, something I don't have to be since we're best friends. Lay off the booze, you're acting like an ass."

Darrell turned to Jenna, his smirk on his face. "Am I being an ass, Jenna baby?"

"A little but it's not the first time." She patted him on the back. "Don't worry, we love you no matter what."

Scowling, Drew grunted and pulled his phone from his pocket. "I don't love you. I think you're being a jerk. Just like always. I need to make a call, I'll be right back."

Jenna captured her husband's wrist as he stood. "Can't it wait? We're having fun."

"It's business."

Darrell snorted into his champagne. "Sure it is. You're practically employee of the month. They ought to give you a plaque. Because nothing is more important than your goddamn job."

Standing, Drew tossed his friend a contemptuous look.

"Shut the fuck up. No one wants to hear you running off at the mouth."

"You mean you don't want to hear me. You don't want to hear anyone, Drew. You don't listen to anyone and you don't give a shit about anyone."

Catching her husband's hand in her own, Jenna slammed down her drink. "Stop it. Both of you. You're acting like children."

Drew nodded to Darrell. "He started it."

"I did no–"

Darrell didn't get any further as Jenna cut him off. "I don't care who started it. I'm ending it. Stop sniping at each other."

Shrugging, Darrell sat back in his chair, smirking at Drew who tugged his hand away from his wife. Leann watched her friend closely as Jenna reluctantly let go of Drew and he walked off. Jenna turned back to the group apologetically. "I'm sorry about that, but when duty calls Drew always answers no matter what. So dedicated."

There was an uncomfortable silence after Drew left, and they were all aware that Jenna wasn't happy that he had. Finally Colin smiled and signaled the waitress. "It's nice when a person loves their job."

Nodding, Jenna tore her gaze away from the door where her husband had exited. "It is, isn't it? What did you say you do, Colin?"

"Orthopedic surgeon."

Darrell laughed and raised his beer bottle. "It's good to be a geek. Now they get all the money and all the chicks."

"Shut up," Jenna hissed through clenched teeth. "You're

embarrassing yourself."

"Just telling the truth." Darrell lifted the last champagne bottle from the bucket and popped it open. "We thought we were so cool in high school but what we didn't know was that the geeks were going to take over the world. Build computers and Twitter and shit. I bust my ass all day long on the ranch and we're lucky to break even at the end of the year. If only I'd worn glasses and been too weak to play sports. My life would have turned out so different."

Leann could feel the tension in Zach's body and see the echoing emotion in the way Colin held himself. Darrell needed to shut the fuck up. Between him, Troy, and Drew it was testosterone central.

"Jesus, Darrell." Jenna shoved at the man's shoulder. "Go get some fresh air or something. These guys are being nice to you and you're being a jerk."

Stumbling to his feet, Darrell picked up the almost full champagne bottle and tucked it under his arm. "That's me. A big old jerk. Just ask my ex-wife. She'll tell you." Swaying slightly, he rounded the table and came to stand by Leann. "Lovely to see you, Leann."

Darrell tottered but managed to exit the ballroom through the same door as Drew. Jenna sighed and dropped her face into her hands. "I'm so sorry about that. Darrell's wife left him a few months ago and he's still upset and bitter about it. He shouldn't have taken his anger out on you two. Hopefully all the drama is over with for the evening."

"It's fine," replied the doctor with a small smile. "I'm sorry to hear about his marriage."

It felt stifling hot in the ballroom and Leann needed a breath of fresh air. There were suddenly too many people in this room. She nudged Zach's arm to get his attention.

"I think I'd like to step outside and get some air."

"Where you go, I go."

She wasn't naive enough to think that was because he couldn't get enough of her scintillating company. It was because he was under orders.

"Then follow me."

✦ ✦ ✦

GALLANTLY ZACH OPENED the door for her and she stepped outside onto a back terrace, the cool breeze caressing her overheated skin. It had been getting warm in the ballroom and this felt lovely. It was fun catching up with her old friends but it was also becoming more intense than she'd anticipated. Between the tragic deaths of her classmates and the personal sniping and backstabbing she was almost wishing she was back in Florida. Almost.

It wasn't unpleasant to stand next to Zach, although his large frame dwarfed her own. He made her feel safe and protected. It might be his job but this was more. He acted as if he was enjoying her company, not just being paid to keep her alive. Perhaps he just wanted to be friends? She'd be disappointed but she could understand. He traveled a lot for his job and he might not want to get involved.

He might just not be into you.

Lots of women tonight had looked Zach up and down but he'd been her date. Now and then she'd felt his hand on the small of her back guiding her and her skin had tingled in response. He was the epitome of tall, dark, and handsome, and after all the time they'd spent together she'd be lying if she said she wasn't smitten. When she'd dressed for the party tonight she'd been thinking of how he might look at her in her outfit. The more time she spent with him the more she liked him.

Had something else been going on this afternoon? Despite pulling back from their kiss, he hadn't liked it when Henry had asked her to sit next to him.

"What made you decide to come to the reunion, Leann? You've been gone a long time."

"Jenna wouldn't take no for an answer," she replied. "Plus, I missed my family, of course."

"Of course," he repeated. "It must be difficult being all alone in another state."

"It can get lonely but I have some good friends there. How about you? Are you settling into Tremont? Weren't you living in Las Vegas before this?"

"I was but the summers were brutal and it was so flat and dry. I like it here better, plus I get to be close to my sisters and my new nephew."

Baby Ryder. One of the major reasons she was thinking of moving back. She didn't want to miss her nephew growing up.

"He is a cutie. I never imagined West as a father, I have to admit."

"I never imagined Gigi as a mom but she's amazing."

The question was out before she could stop it. "Do you think about settling down and having a family?"

Leann wanted to run and hide. It was an incredibly personal

query and they weren't even on a real date. He was being forced to escort her here.

"Someday. I'm concentrating on getting my career going right now."

Zach checked his phone and then tucked it back into his jacket pocket, which reminded her that he was waiting for news about the case.

"Have you heard anything? You know…about Bitty and Carole?"

He shook his head. "We're waiting on forensics but I doubt they'll give us much. Right now I'm concentrating on the psychology of the killer since we have so little physical evidence."

"You have a theory."

He didn't answer immediately but eventually he nodded. "I do. At first this felt like revenge but it isn't quite right. The cases I've seen in the past were because the victims bullied the killer and the wounds festered over a long period of time, creating a compulsion to even the score, so to speak. According to you and some other people I've spoken with, Carole and Bitty might have been popular but they weren't cruel. Which leads me to the conclusion that it's not revenge the killer wants. This is about envy. The killer believes that these women didn't deserve what they had and that he has received less than his share. It's a different motivation for settling the score. And that theory puts you right in the path of this guy."

Jason had mentioned to Leann that Zach had taken on the role of profiler in the consulting firm and that he was damn good at it.

"I'm sorry you have to babysit me. I'm sure there are other

things you'd rather be doing than this."

Leann wasn't prepared for the intensity of his reply. Leaning down so they were almost nose to nose, he placed a finger under her chin so she was looking into his blue eyes.

"There is no place I'd rather be and nothing more important."

Her mouth had fallen open and she was struggling to speak when the door to the ballroom flew open and Jenna stood there, her brows pinched together.

"Is Drew out here? He never came back from that phone call and I'm starting to get a little worried. He's been drinking quite a bit tonight."

Because she was so close to Zach she could instantly feel the tensing of his body. His hand fell away and she felt bereft as he took a step backward, putting space between them.

"We'll help you find him," Zach replied. "Where have you checked so far?"

Chapter Ten

THE PARTY WAS over. Guests were filtering out one by one until there were only about two dozen of them left. Drew wasn't among them.

Leann's gaze ran over the ballroom. "The last time I saw him was when he left after our champagne toast. That was quite a while ago."

Jenna's front teeth worried her lower lip. "That's the last time I saw him too, but I thought he was just having fun with the guys. I wonder if he left and went back to work."

"Would he do that?" Leann asked, craning her neck to see over the crowd.

Jenna groaned and checked her phone. "When work calls, Drew jumps but he'd let me know and there are no messages. He has to be here."

"I don't see him," Zach said, "But there are several other conference rooms in this part of the hotel. Maybe Drew and a few buddies found an empty one and are talking about the old days? I can go check."

"Me too," Leann, offered seeing how worried Jenna was and rightfully so. Drew had been drinking quite a bit earlier. Not as much as Darrell, but still a lot.

"We'll all go," Jenna replied, whirling on her high heel. "If he's really drunk I may need some help getting him to the car. Tomorrow morning I'm going to have the kids practice their band instruments."

Giggling, Leann let Zach lead the way. "That should teach him to drink too much."

Jenna rolled her eyes. "He never learns. He did this at the company Christmas party last year too."

Zach's hand came up to cup Leann's elbow. "Stick with me. I don't want to let you out of my sight."

She didn't question him, simply following his lead. The easy smile he'd been wearing earlier was gone and his expression had sobered. It was fascinating how quickly his moods changed.

The convention center area of the hotel was a labyrinth of hallways and doors that seem to lead to nowhere and then suddenly Leann was back where she started. Or maybe not. The beige carpeting and ubiquitous walls all looked exactly the same. If Drew was back here drunk, she could completely understand how he might not have been able to find his way out.

Leann pointed to the long hallway. "Have we checked this one yet?"

Zach turned and looked at the door behind them. "I don't think so. I don't think we've been in this hallway. I don't remember that emergency fire alarm."

Jenna nodded. "I think you're right. There are only three doors here and then we're done."

"I doubt we're going to find anything," Jenna said with a sigh, heading down the hall to the third door. "It's really quiet back here. If Drew were in one of these rooms I'd guess he'd be whooping it up with his friends. We'd hear it for sure."

Not if Drew was passed out from too much to drink.

Leann stuck her head into the conference room and flipped on the light. Empty but for a large table and several chairs. Perhaps Drew was outside? Passed out in the car or on a bench? Maybe he'd booked a room so he didn't have to drive home?

Leann turned to Zach who was shaking his head. He hadn't found anything either. "I don't see him. Should we check with the front–"

A scream ripped through the silence and then Jenna backed out of the conference room, falling backward onto the carpet. Her hands were over her face and she was repeating Drew's name over and over like a mantra. Leann quickly fell to her knees beside her best friend. She wrapped her arms around the crying and shaking woman as Zach ducked into the room Jenna had just vacated to see what had her in hysterics.

"Jenna, what's going on? You need to calm down for a second and tell me what's wrong."

Zach's hand on her shoulder pulled Leann's attention to him. She looked up and her stomach twisted into a knot at the bleak expression on his face.

"He's dead."

Jenna was rocking back and forth, weeping uncontrollably and Leann tried to keep her own voice calm even as panic flared inside of her. Zach looked serious.

"Drew?" Leann asked in a hushed tone. "Are you sure?"

Zach nodded, his face pale as he retrieved his phone from his front pocket and handed it to Leann. "Call the police while I secure the scene. It's going to be a long night."

✦ ✦ ✦

THE COPS HAD cordoned off the remaining guests at the reunion into a conference room while they combed the crime scene and the ballroom for evidence.

Leann was trying to comfort Jenna while Zach patiently asked the woman several questions, mostly getting tears as a response. He felt great sympathy for Jenna, especially since she had been the one to find her husband's dead body – that was something no spouse should have to endure – but he also needed a few answers. The first twenty-four hours after a crime were the most important while leads were still fresh.

"Tell me a little about the relationship of Drew and Troy," Zach tried again, taking a different path. "It appeared that they were arguing about you."

Jenna flushed and nodded.

"Was that the first time punches were thrown? Have they fought before?"

"In high school." Jenna's reply was soft. "But that was so long ago. We haven't seen Troy in years."

Zach scribbled a few notes. "You haven't spoken with him in all that time?"

She shook her head, a fresh round of tears starting. "No, I haven't even thought about him since graduation. Is he still here? Have you talked to him?"

"Not yet but I will," Zach promised, his attention captured by a movement out of the corner of his eye. The shift leader of the crime scene unit had arrived. "Could you excuse me for a moment?"

"Can I take her home?" Leann asked, her gaze pleading. "She's in no condition to answer any more questions."

Zach wasn't getting anywhere so he might as well let Jenna go home and get some rest. Leann, however, was another story all together. He beckoned to Leann and they stepped away out of Jenna's hearing.

"Jenna can go but I will have more questions tomorrow. Both of you need to be under police protection. I'll send officers home with you and Jenna since I need to stay here. In the morning we need to discuss security arrangements in more detail."

Leann looked about as thrilled at that news as he'd expected.

"It would be futile to argue, I assume?" she asked. "I can't imagine why someone would want me dead, Zach."

She was incredibly naive or maybe she was just playing innocent. "You can't? Are you sure, Leann? Because you were born with a silver spoon in your mouth and grew up practically the princess of this little town. You can't imagine how someone might be envious of that?"

Zach hadn't meant for it to come out that coarsely but from her pale face he could tell she'd listened. She had to know that she was a target.

She crossed her arms over her chest in a protective gesture. "I guess I can see that."

"I didn't mean to–"

She held up her hand. "No, I get it. It's just not something I think about much. My family is just my family. We're not royalty."

"You're local royalty," Zach pressed. "You've been lucky and other people might resent that. We need to be cautious. I can't let anything happen to you."

She nodded but didn't say anything else, simple walking back to Jenna and placing an arm around her friend's shoulders.

"I'm going to have an officer escort both of you back to your residences," Zach said, knowing he'd be here all night. He'd have to trust someone else to look after Leann, at least for a few hours, and he didn't like that at all.

Jenna gave him a look of alarm. "Do you think we're in danger?"

"I think we need to be overly protective until we know more," Zach replied in his best soothing voice that he'd perfected after many years in personal security. "Tomorrow we'll talk again."

Leann picked up her purse from the chair. "Are you ready to go, Jenna?"

Her friend nodded. "Let me just run to the ladies room for a second. I'll be right back."

Turning to Zach when Jenna was out of earshot, Leann's eyes teared up and a sob escaped her throat.

"This has been the most horrible night. I don't know what to say to Jenna to make this any better."

"There is nothing you can say, Leann. Just be there for her, which you're already doing. She's going to need the love and support of her family and friends."

"She has mine and so many others as well." She bit her lip and wiped away a stray tear from her cheek. "How could no one have heard anything? That's what I don't understand."

"That's not surprising. The conference room is quite a ways from the ballroom," Zach pointed out. "Also the music was loud, and with all the people talking and laughing, they would have had to make quite the ruckus to have attracted anyone's attention."

"How…how…did he die?"

Leann hadn't actually seen inside the conference room, which as far as Zach was concerned was an extremely good thing. It had been a grisly scene.

"I'm not telling you anything that won't be in the papers tomorrow. The medical examiner will need to do an autopsy but the preliminary report is that Drew Marshall died by exsanguination. His carotid artery was severed with what we think was a broken champagne bottle but we don't know for sure yet."

Zach had seen the bottle next to the body and at first he'd simply thought Drew had dropped it when he'd been killed. But then he'd seen the blood on the jagged edge… It had been the murder weapon, he was sure of it.

Leann's face had turn a nasty shade of gray. "Darrell had an entire bottle of champagne tucked under his arm when he left the ballroom. He was pretty drunk, too."

"We'll be talking to him," Zach said grimly. "But we'll also get the pieces of bottle fingerprinted. If he touched it, we'll know."

"And Troy too?"

"Troy as well. I need to account for everyone's whereabouts at the time of death."

Jenna exited the ladies room but hovered near the doorway, seemingly eager to leave. Leann nodded to her friend and then turned back to Zach.

"I should get her home. I'm hoping Jenna can get a little rest tonight."

"I'll be by to talk to her again tomorrow. You too. I'll need to get your statement."

She smiled slightly. "My statement is your statement. We were together pretty much the entire evening."

"True, but you might have noticed something I didn't." The uniformed officer that was going to follow the women home hurried into the room. "Harn, thanks for helping with this. I need you to follow Ms. Anderson and Mrs. Marshall home and make sure they get there safely, okay?"

The young cop nodded eagerly. "Will do. Should I come back here after?"

"No, you are to stay outside of Mrs. Marshall's house until another officer comes to relieve you." He placed his hand on Leann's shoulder. "I'll send a unit to your friend's house as well for you. See you in the morning."

Leann murmured her goodbye and Zach watched as she and Jenna left, escorted by Harn. This entire case was taking a strange turn. The victimology had started out straightforward. Two popular girls who might have ostracized someone back in high school. But now the captain of the football team was dead. An up close and personal kind of death. Cutting wasn't a detached method of killing. From the look of the crime scene, this person had a lot of rage inside of them. More than with the other two murders. What did it all mean?

Shoving the small notebook into his jacket pocket, Zach went in search of the medical examiner and the crime scene crew. So many questions and hardly any answers.

Chapter Eleven

THE YOUNG FEMALE assistant ushered Zach into his brother-in-law Mayor West Anderson's office. Zach's appearance wasn't a surprise as West had asked him to stop by on his way back to the station.

"Come in."

Zach pushed open the heavy oak door and stepped into West's office. Anderson was all business normally but he did have a photo of his wife Gigi – Zach's sister – and their new baby son on the desk. The new daddy looked like he could use some extra sleep.

To Zach's surprise, Jason Anderson was sitting on the edge of his little brother's desk. A cup of coffee was in one hand and a file folder in the other.

"Come in," West said again. "Help yourself to some coffee, although I should warn you that I made it. My assistant is a tea drinker and hers is even worse."

Helping himself to the coffee, Zach added plenty of cream and sugar. Just in case it really was bad. "It can't be any worse than what we have at the office. That stuff will strip the varnish from your furniture."

Laughing, Jason took another sip of his own coffee. "Bad coffee is part of law enforcement. It's practically a tradition."

Zach settled into the chair across from West. "So you wanted to see me?"

Jason rolled his eyes at Zach's tone. "West wanted an update and I thought it would be easier for you to update me and him all at once."

"I appreciate that." Zach rubbed at his tired eyes. "I didn't get much sleep last night."

Actually he'd slept zero hours.

Folding his hands on the desk in front of him, West's expression was somber. "I don't like murder in Tremont and I like a killer on the loose even less. Do we have any suspects?"

"A bunch of them. Too many, in fact. Pretty much everyone at the reunion last night, although luckily most of the guests had left before the estimated time of death. It should make things a little easier. I'm headed back to the office now to start putting together a report of everyone's whereabouts—the ones I have, anyway. There are still several people to be accounted for."

Jason picked up a piece of paper with handwriting on it. "Troy Wallace and Darrell Madison are the main suspects, correct? Have you talked to them yet?"

Zach had a feeling Jason already knew the answer to that. Who had done the talking? The medical examiner? A patrolman? "We can't find them. We have a BOLO out for both. We'll get them and bring them in. However, I think we need to act cautiously here. While they are suspects for Drew's death, they don't have much connection to Carole or Bitty."

"But you're looking for one?" West asked.

Rubbing his chin, Zach nodded. "Yes, but it's early in the investigation. Things can change quickly as you know."

West sat back in the oversized leather chair. "That's true. Have we heard anything from the lab?"

"The lab is working on the broken champagne bottle and if there are prints, that should point us in the right direction."

Jason pulled out his phone and began typing into it. "The state lab can take a long time to get you those results. I'll see what pressure I can put on them."

"I'd appreciate that."

There was more West wanted to say. Zach could see it in the other man's eyes. What was holding him back? Something was definitely going on.

Fiddling with a pencil, West took his time before speaking. "My sister was there last night."

Ah, this is about Leann.

"She was," Zach confirmed, instantly wary. He didn't know where West was going with this line of questioning but he was smart enough to know this meeting wasn't a casual sit down about Drew Marshall's death. It was much more.

"Jenna is a good friend of Leann's."

Zach could only agree. Again. "That was apparent from how they interacted."

"I'm sure she's devastated for Jenna."

West was playing Captain Obvious this morning and Zach hadn't had a wink of sleep. He wasn't in tip-top shape to play this game but he could make vague, obvious statements too.

"She is, of course."

West nodded. "It's just that...well...Jason and I were talking…"

The older brother's head popped up and he grinned, shaking his head. "No, you don't. Do not drag me into this with you. This is all your show. I'm staying out of it."

Was Zach about to get the "stay away from my sister" speech? No one knew the "guy code" better than he did. Leann was the little sister and that meant she was off limits. End of story. That's why he'd been staying as far away from her as possible despite his growing attraction. She wasn't just gorgeous, she was also smart and funny too.

"We don't have to do this," Zach said. "I get it. Leann's out of bounds."

West's cheeks turned pink and he shifted in his seat. "It's not that we don't like you, Zach. We do. Shit, you're family, man. This isn't a lecture about keeping your grubby paws off of our sister."

But that's exactly what it was.

"But I need to do that."

Apparently Jason had had enough of his brother's fumbling. "As far as I'm concerned, all you need to do is keep Leann safe. Anything else is between you and her."

West scowled at Jason. "Of course you need to stick close to Leann and keep her safe, but not too close, if you know what I mean."

Zach kind of enjoyed West's discomfiture. "You mean close like you are with Gigi? My sister? Like that close?"

Laughing, Jason stood and refilled his coffee. "He's got you there, little brother. You're doing all manner of things to his sister."

"We're married," West sputtered, the color on his cheeks deepening to red. "It's different."

"You weren't always married," Zach pointed out. "The only saving grace you had when I met you is that you were keeping Gigi safe. Otherwise I would have pounded you into the ground."

Jason lounged back against the credenza and grinned. "I can't begin to tell you how much fun this conversation is. West warning Zach off for exactly what he himself did. Pot and kettle."

Zach shook his head. "Not exactly. I haven't touched your sister."

"Do you want to?" West growled, the pencil he'd been playing with snapping in two pieces.

"Let's take a breath here," Jason suggested, straightening from his perch and settling into a chair next to Zach. "We're all family and we need to start acting like it. Zach, if you want to start something with Leann then don't let me or this asshole stop you. God knows you're better than most of the guys she's dated, not that we've seen all of them since she moved but we've seen and heard enough. We know you'll do everything in your power to keep her safe and treat her well. Right, West?"

The younger brother sighed. "Right. We know that you're a good guy. It's just she's our little sister…"

"I get that," Zach replied quickly, not sure he wanted to have this discussion. He was attracted as hell to Leann and there were times he thought the feelings were returned but he couldn't be positive. "Listen, I'm not sure anything is going on between us and while I'm protecting her isn't the best time to find out.

Maybe after we catch this guy she and I can talk about it."

West sat back in his chair, seemingly satisfied with Zach's response. "That's all I'm saying. Take your time. Don't rush into anything."

"What West is saying," Jason replied as if his brother hadn't spoken at all, "is that this is none of our fucking business and you two are grown adults who don't need us to tell you what to do. But if you break her heart? You'll wish you'd never been born. Got it?"

West had frowned when Jason started speaking but now he was grinning ear to ear. These Anderson boys were a real piece of work. West was lucky that Gigi was so happy. Zach wouldn't mind reminding the mayor that he was twice as big and could put a hurt on West that he wouldn't forget in a hurry.

"Message received. Are we done here?"

The two brothers nodded and Jason stood, following Zach out onto the sidewalk.

"I meant what I said back there. Don't worry about West. He's always been like this, overly protective of Leann. They've butted heads more times than I can count but his heart is in the right place."

Zach studied his employer and the sentiment seemed genuine, which surprised him. Jason didn't seem to have an issue with the foster kid romancing his sister. That was a shock.

"Right now it's all business," Zach responded. "Your sister is probably just tolerating me at this point."

Jason palmed his car keys. "Time will tell. Call me later and update me. Don't worry about calling West. I'll keep him in the loop. Just keep my sister alive. I don't care what you have to do.

Don't let her out of your sight."

That was the plan. "I'm headed there right now."

Romance was tempting but it was going to have to take a back burner to protecting Leann. If anyone wanted to hurt her they were going to have to go through him.

✦ ✦ ✦

JASON STROLLED BACK into his brother's office after Zach drove away. He and West needed to have a talk. As usual, he wasn't seeing the big picture here and Jason was going to have to draw him a map.

"I thought you'd left," West looked up from his paperwork in surprise. "Have you come here to tell me that you only temporarily lost your mind and that you warned Zach away from our sister after all?"

Flopping down into a guest chair, Jason had to rein in his impatience. Hopefully once he explained all of this to his brother he'd be on board.

"I have not," Jason replied flatly. "What I have come back to do is straighten your ass out. Now listen to me. Do you or do you not want Leann to move back home?"

"I do," West answered, tapping his pencil—a new one—against the desk. "We all do."

"That's right. Now follow me and think about it before you shoot off at the mouth again. If Leann and Zach become a couple, what do you think might happen?"

West's mouth fell open and his eyes widened.

"Exactly," Jason stated, a smile coming to his own face. "There's a decent chance Leann will move home. She gets a good man to take care of her and we get her back in Tremont. Do you follow me?"

His younger brother threw up his hands. "How did I not think of this myself? It's fucking brilliant."

"Don't beat yourself up too much. I didn't think of it myself until a few days ago, but this could be just what we need to lure her back home. I think she likes Zach a lot and I know he likes her. You can tell when they're in the same room with each other. Now we just need to encourage that and what better way than to push them together? I told Zach not to let her out of his sight."

"They'll either fall in love or end up hating each other."

"Let's hope it's the former and not the latter. Then she might never come back."

West stroked his chin. "Do you really think they like each other?"

"No doubt in my mind. The way they were looking at each other at the memorial service was obvious. They're attracted but Leann's too shy to make the first move and Zach wouldn't do it because of me and his job. Now that I've lifted that barrier, hopefully he'll let his feelings be known."

Smiling, West pulled a bottle of whiskey out of his bottom drawer plus two glasses. "Damn, this is going to be great. Leann finally coming home. It's been too long. You're a genius."

"Damn right I am."

Zach and Leann would fall in love, get married, and settle down in Tremont. They just needed a little bit of encouragement and the plan was foolproof.

Chapter Twelve

LEANN'S MOTHER HAD drilled it into her daughter's head almost from birth that one never showed up at the home of a bereaved friend empty-handed. Therefore, Leann was standing in Jenna's dining room holding a tray of meats and cheeses she'd had made up at the grocery store along with a large bowl of homemade chocolate pudding. Homemade by Dizzy, actually. That girl had a way with desserts that defied logic. Leann had thought Jenna's kids might want some old-fashioned "comfort" food and Dizzy had been happy to have someone to cook for.

Jenna and Drew had two children, a boy and a girl. Every year at Christmas time, like clockwork, Leann received a photo card from the family featuring them all smiling and wearing matching holiday sweaters. There wouldn't be any more of those – at least not with Drew.

Those poor kids.

Having grown up in a happy but busy family, Leann couldn't begin to imagine what those children were going through, having lost their father. It was times like this life reminded everyone that it wasn't fair.

The house was full of people, most of whom Leann recognized but a few she didn't. Jenna sat in the living room surrounded by family and friends. The two children were nowhere in sight but Leann vividly remembered being a pre-teenager. They were probably holed up in their room with their friends. Adults were not cool.

"Leann, can I take those for you and put them on the table?"

Whirling around, Leann was face to face with her mother. Eileen Anderson wore the gentlest expression as if afraid to spook her only daughter, and for good reason. Leann had been actively avoiding her parents since she'd hit town Thursday morning. She didn't want to walk the usual question gauntlet. Was she seeing anyone? If not, would she consider moving back and joining one of the family businesses? She simply wasn't ready to discuss her possible plans to return to Tremont. If Leann had her way, she'd simply show up at Sunday dinner one day and announce she'd bought a house and moved in under the cover of darkness.

Relinquishing the tray to her mother, Leann followed and placed the pudding bowl down on the table that was already laden with food. Apparently, everyone in Tremont knew the adage about showing up empty-handed.

"The pudding looks good. Did you make it?" Eileen smiled at her daughter's rueful expression as she gave her a hug. "Dizzy made it, didn't she? She's certainly an excellent cook so I bet it's wonderful."

"She offered and it was her kitchen, so…"

"You could have come home and made it," her mother reminded her gently.

Leann could have but that would have meant dealing with

her parents. “I didn’t want to bother you.”

Eileen swept a strand of Leann’s hair away from her face. Her mother had the same red hair, although it was streaked with gray now. The boys had inherited their father’s dark hair.

“You’re no bother, sweetheart. We would have been happy to have you stay with us.”

Nervously, Leann smoothed down her emerald green shift dress. It gave her hands something to do. “Dizzy’s is in town and she lets me use her car.”

“We have several vehicles on the ranch but I suppose you have a point. The ranch is a much longer drive into town.”

Slowly but surely, Eileen was boxing Leann in, pushing her to say the great unsaid. A change in subject was imperative. “So, is Dad here too?”

Her mother nodded. “Along with your cousins Noah and Easton. I have no idea what the others are doing but expect they’ll make an appearance at some point.” Eileen’s gaze darted around the room. “Did Dizzy come with you?”

“She’s giving a painting class for seniors at the community center this afternoon.”

Eileen beamed as she rearranged the food on the table to make more room. “I know that she does that as a volunteer and doesn’t get paid a dime. She’s a sweet one. I can’t believe some lucky young man hasn’t swept her off her feet.”

Talking about someone else took the heat off of Leann, although she was only delaying the inevitable. She and her parents had the exact same conversation every time she came home and this time she might have different answers, but strangely enough it didn’t make it any easier. If anything, it made it more difficult because that's when the torrent of questions would come about when she was moving and where she would live. Would she work for the family?

Seemingly out of nowhere, Easton reached over his aunt's back and snagged a piece of cheese. "Who's a sweet one? It can't be Leann. Not with that sourpuss."

Nothing had changed since they were children. They still loved to give each other a hard time and insults were at the top of the list. Easton needed to be careful because Leann knew a hell of a lot more about him than he knew about her.

Elbowing her cousin, Leann made a show of clearing her throat. "I'll have you know that I am very sweet. Now be nice to your aunt and stop crowding her." She peered around Easton. "Where's your annoying twin?"

Noah was six minutes older than Easton.

"He had to take a call so he stepped outside."

Eileen slapped at Easton's hand as he reached across her again. "Have some manners and get a plate. As for who we were talking about, it was Dizzy, of course. She's one of the sweetest girls in Tremont. I can't believe she's still single."

"I can," Easton declared. "She's strange as hell. It was raining the other day and I was driving down Maple Street and I saw her walking so I stopped to offer her a ride, which I thought was the gentlemanly thing to do. She refused my kind offer and said that rain was – and I quote – cleansing her soul. Whatever the hell that means. So I drove on and she got soaked. Then there was that time–"

Eileen held up her hand. "We get the idea. Dizzy is one of a kind, a truly unique individual, and she does some things that might seem a little out there to other people. She does, however, have a heart of gold and she is quite talented. Creative types don't always conform to social norms."

Easton snorted. "She's looking at social norms in the rear-view mirror, Auntie. But you're right, she is a good person. I know she does a lot of volunteer work for the community. Now if you will excuse me I need to get back to the office. Anderson Industries won't run itself, you know. Anytime you want to join us and do some real work, Leann, let me know. We could use a corporate psychologist in the HR department."

More of this. She should have expected it. "Then you should hire one."

Easton dropped a kiss on Leann's cheek. "You won't be able to hold out forever."

"Watch me."

Leann watched as Easton bounded out of the front door, hurrying to get back to the office.

"I think the more we push you, the more you push back," Eileen observed shrewdly. "Maybe if we stop asking, you'll come home on your own."

Feeling the heat suffuse her cheeks, Leann wasn't sure how to respond. All of those expectations. What it meant to be an Anderson. It didn't help that she was the only female of this generation. It was a shit-ton of baggage to be carrying around and she was completely free from it in her adopted state of Florida.

"Maybe. That's a big decision."

Her mother nodded. "It is and don't think that we don't realize it. You have a friends and a career down there and it would be hard to leave, but we do miss you, sweetheart. I hope you're planning to come to Sunday dinner. Bring Zach with you, too."

Sunday dinner at the Anderson house was legendary and a child didn't miss it unless they had a damn good reason. Leann had always planned to attend.

"I'll be there and I think I have to bring him. He's my bodyguard."

Eileen gifted her with a wide smile. "We can have a nice long visit. You can tell me about you and your Zach."

Huh?

"I don't know what you're talking about, Mom. Zach is just doing his job. There's nothing going on between us."

Eileen fussed with a stack of napkins at the end of the table. "You've spent a lot of time with him lately."

The speed of light had nothing on the speed of gossip in Tremont. "I did but I would hardly call him *my Zach*. We danced and talked. As of now, there are no wedding plans. He was my escort so he could question the reunion guests without spooking them, plus as I said he's protecting me. Although he isn't at the moment. I'm being followed around by a deputy who is sitting outside in his cruiser intimidating everyone."

It had been beyond embarrassing being driven to the wake by the police.

"Don't wait too long, sweetheart. Zach is what we called a stone fox back in my day."

Pressing her hand to her warm cheeks, Leann couldn't suppress a giggle. "Mother, please. He's my brother-in-law. Sort of."

Eileen nudged her daughter. "Looks like there's a break in the crowd around Jenna. Now might be a good time to go over and pay your respects. I'll be in the kitchen so come by before you leave."

"I will, Mom." Leann began to turn away but stopped, emotion swelling inside of her as she gazed at Jenna's tearstained face. Somehow, some way she needed to heal the rift she'd caused by leaving. She and her parents were too wary and scared, always waiting for the next strike. The toxic pattern had to be stopped in its tracks and it started now. Today. "And Mom...I love you."

Eileen smiled and patted Leann on the cheek. "I never doubted that. I love you, too. So very much. We all do."

It was a start.

Chapter Thirteen

ZACH AND JASON were tucked into a booth in the back of the half-empty diner. The lunch rush was over but it was still too early for dinner. It was the perfect time to meet and have a piece of pie and a cup of coffee.

Jason took notes on his tablet. "I can do that. I'll have Jared run the names of attendees for any priors. That won't take long. Anything else?"

Zach shifted uncomfortably on the vinyl seat. This was a small town and the people were close, protective of one another. "I'd like to get some background on the Marshalls. Finances, social media, that sort of thing."

Jason's brows shot up. "Are you leaning away from your two suspects?"

Holding his hand up, Zach shook his head. "Not in the least. I think they're definitely worth a look. Frankly, there were several people at that reunion who could have been carrying a grudge against Drew. From the what I've been able to find out, he was kind of a bully back in the day and humans have long memories. But investigating him and the women is my standard operating procedure. The more I know the deceased, the more I can get into the motivations of the killer. I'm still not sold on the revenge theory. It just doesn't feel right."

"It's a good idea to check them out," Jason approved, tapping at the screen. "Especially when you have so many suspects. Just because someone wasn't invited to the reunion doesn't mean they weren't the perpetrator. He could have been waiting until the reunion to do the deed, thinking that suspicion would be on everyone but him."

"You keep saying 'he'," Zach laughed, digging into his apple pie. "Do you know something I don't? It could very well be a female. Drew had a string of broken hearts in high school from what I've been told and the other victims were female. There could be a grudge there. Revenge is male, envy is female."

"Just an assumption based on the mode of death. Drew should have been able to easily overpower a woman who was wielding that champagne bottle, plus the strength needed to strangle Bitty."

"I'd normally agree with you but Drew had been drinking all night. I think he could have been overpowered by someone weaker, especially if they had the element of surprise."

Jason signaled for more coffee. "That's a good point. I'm anxious to hear what the medical examiner has to say about his blood alcohol level."

"I want to hear from the crime lab if they found any evidence that might lead to narrowing down the suspect list. As it is I've got over two dozen possible suspects plus the hotel staff. That doesn't include your theory that someone slipped in to the hotel and can't be accounted for. We'll know more when we hear from the lab. I've got my fingers crossed that the champagne bottle had fingerprints."

Something had to break and soon.

✦ ✦ ✦

"I CAN'T BELIEVE she had the nerve to show her face here," Jenna hissed from her perch on the couch, her gaze sweeping the room full of people and zeroing in on one particular woman. "She has absolutely no respect."

Leann looked around, confused for a moment as to whom Jenna was referring to, but then she saw Nicole Quincy placing a pie on the dining room table. Dressed in white pants and a peach blouse, the brunette was quite pretty. Leann didn't remember seeing her last night at the reunion.

"That was fifteen years ago," Leann reasoned. "I think it's actually kind of nice that she stopped by to pay her respects. I'm sure she's moved on from having a crush on Drew."

It didn't appear that Jenna had though from the way she was seething, her eyes following Nicole's every movement. "She slept with my husband."

Only kind of true.

"Drew wasn't your husband then. He wasn't even your boyfriend at the time. You two had broken up over some reason that I bet you don't even recall. You went to the homecoming dance with someone else too."

Reasoning with her friend wasn't going well. Jerking her gaze away from Nicole, Jenna rounded on Leann. "Traitor. Are you taking her side?"

Jenna was emotionally overwrought and obviously not thinking clearly. Leann remembered homecoming night well and

Jenna had been in the back seat of a Camry with another boy.

"Are there sides to take fifteen years later over one school dance? You and Drew sowed some wild oats and then you settled down together. He chose you and you chose him. The fling they had that night can't compare to the life you and he had."

A fresh spate of tears rolled down Jenna's cheeks and Leann pushed the tissue box closer.

"You just don't understand." Jenna shook her head, dabbing at her swollen eyes. "You've never loved or been loved by a man. If you had, you would be on my side."

Ouch. That was unnecessarily cruel.

Her friend was grieving so Leann wanted to be considerate. Understanding. Gracious.

"You shouldn't let something that happened so long ago mar your memories of Drew and the life you built together. No one can take those from you."

Shrugging, Jenna grabbed another tissue from the box. "Like I said before, you really don't get it. Maybe someday you will."

Mentally counting to ten, Leann took a deep breath. It wasn't worth pursuing and none of this was about her, anyway. But it did remind her why she and Jenna had drifted apart after graduation.

"This is a lovely turnout," Leann said, wanting to change the subject. "Drew was certainly well thought of in Tremont."

"Someone hated my husband enough to kill him," the widow said sharply, her eyes narrowing as she took in the room full of people. "Someone looked him in the eye and then killed him."

Jenna had always been something of a drama queen but considering the circumstances Leann was willing to give her friend a huge amount of latitude. If Jenna wanted to scream and stomp her feet that was fine with Leann.

"That's…true," Leann conceded cautiously. Was Jenna planning to confront someone right here at the wake? "But dwelling on it isn't going to make you feel better. I'm sure Zach will have the guilty party behind bars very soon."

Jenna blew her nose again. "Everyone thinks it's Troy or Darrell but I have another theory. I think it's one of the kids that Drew used to bully. They came to the reunion to kill him as revenge. That's why they killed Carole and Bitty too."

Leann didn't like to speak ill of the dead but Drew had played some nasty jokes on several of the so-called "geeks" in high school. Carole and Bitty hadn't done anything overtly cruel but certainly someone might have taken their actions as a slight.

"Whoever it is, Zach will find him," she said in her most soothing tone. "This isn't his and Jason's first murder case. Not even close."

Bursting into tears, Jenna buried her face in the crumpled tissue. "Nothing is going to bring him back."

Wrapping her arm around her friend, Leann tried to comfort Jenna as best she could. What the woman said was true. Drew was gone.

"Go ahead and cry," Leann urged, patting Jenna on the back. "Get it all out. I'm here for you. We're all here for you."

A whole room full of people just to support Jenna. And one of them might just be the killer.

Chapter Fourteen

"HOW WOULD YOU like that cooked?" the waiter asked Leann as he retrieved the two menus from the table and tucked them under his arm. She and Zach were dining on a Saturday night at one of the better restaurants in Tremont, which meant that the place was packed. The sound of voices and the tinkling of glasses drifted in the air as well as the aroma of freshly baked bread and spices. Her stomach growled in anticipation and she placed a hand over her abdomen, hoping that the din of the other diners drowned it out.

"Medium, please," she replied and he hurried back into the kitchen, leaving her and Zach on their own. He'd called while she was at Jenna's with an invitation to dinner and she had been happy to accept. Her thoughts had kept turning to him all day long. She was so used to having him around that when he was gone it seemed strange.

"A woman who orders a steak and potato…I like it," Zach approved with a grin. "Let's make a pact that no matter how full we are from dinner we'll definitely order dessert."

"They make a terrific chocolate mousse here. You should try it."

He had let her pick the restaurant after revealing he was starved because he'd missed lunch. This steakhouse had some of the largest portions in a three-county area.

"I will. Now tell me all about your day."

It sucked.

"I want to hear about yours. I'm sure it was much more interesting."

Zach shook his head. "I don't know about that. How about we take turns? You first?"

Taking a deep breath, Leann wasn't sure where to start. "That sounds like a fair deal. I went over to Jenna's today, along with half of Tremont it seemed like. I feel so terrible for her. She's angry and depressed. A little scared too. She was even mad about one of Drew's old girlfriends coming by to pay her respects."

Now that she'd sat with Jenna's remarks for a few hours, they'd hurt more than she realized. Leann was well aware that in her friend's state of mind she was going to hit out at the nearest target – and it didn't matter who it was.

Zach's brows pulled down as he fumbled with his phone and scrolled through a document or list. "Who was that? Wait. Was it Nicole Quincy?"

"It was. How do you know about her?" Playfully, she tried to get a look at the screen of his phone. "Do you have some sort of cheat sheet on there?"

Laughing, he tucked it back into his jacket pocket. "I was reading through the statements from the reunion guests today and she was mentioned a few times. Apparently she and Drew had a fling in high school and he dumped her. A few people thought she might want revenge."

Frowning, Leann took a sip of her red wine. "That wasn't how I remember it. They had a fling on homecoming night. After which she immediately started dating some super hot guy from a neighboring high school. Then she moved away during Christmas holidays and spent several years abroad from what I heard. I don't think revenge was ever on her mind."

It was funny how people could have wildly different perspective of the exact same events.

"She's back in town now and I've added her to my list to talk to. I didn't see her at the reunion last night so the entire conversation might be for nothing. You said she was at the wake today?"

Leann nodded. "She was and Jenna was beside herself with anger, but then she was super-emotional about everything. I think if something burned in the kitchen she would have had a meltdown. She was never one to hide her feelings, which in this case I think is a good thing. She'll get it all out and won't be bottling things up in an unhealthy way. Did you stop by there today?"

"I meant to but the day got crazy. I figured that it was probably better that I put my nose to the grindstone and find the killer. That's the only thing that's going to give her any closure. So what else did you do?"

She rubbed her fingers on the hem of the cloth napkin. "I saw some of my family. Mom wanted to make sure I was coming to Sunday dinner tomorrow. Which of course means you're invited unless you decide to send me with one of the deputies."

"I'd love to go. Your mother is an excellent cook and I think the deputies can have a day off tomorrow. You'll be with me."

His voice had deepened at the end and his tone was positively possessive. Looking into each other's eyes, there was so much unsaid between them. The attraction wasn't something she'd imagined. It was a real, palpable thing. Whatever reason he'd pulled back it wasn't because he didn't find her attractive. His warm gaze had swept her head to toe tonight and the appraisal had been all male appreciation. He'd liked what he'd seen. A warm glow radiated from her middle all the way to the tips of her fingers. It had been too long since she'd met a man that interested her this much.

The waiter slid their salads in front of them.

Zach lifted his wine glass. "Here's a toast to finding killers and your mother's amazing cooking."

Clinking her glass on his, she smiled. "I'll drink to that. Now if I could just get my brothers to stay out of my business things would be perfect. They tend to stick their nose where it doesn't belong."

Zach choked on his wine and she almost jumped out of her chair to slap him on the back.

"Are you okay?"

Holding up his hand, he nodded, clearing his throat several times. "I'm okay. It just went down the wrong pipe. It's fine."

She signaled to the waiter. "Let's get you some more water. Do you need anything else?"

Shaking his head, Zach chuckled, picking up his fork and digging into his salad. "Really, it's all good. Did you do anything else today?"

✦ ✦ ✦

ZACH HAD ALMOST choked to death when Leann mentioned her brothers meddling in her business. It reminded him that West didn't want him getting too close to his sister. With Zach's growing attraction to Leann, that directive was getting much more difficult to follow. All of his instincts were telling him that this woman was special and he'd be a fool not to pursue a relationship with her.

Honestly, it wasn't West's business and clearly Leann would be livid if she knew about his meeting with her brother this morning. Zach wasn't about to tell her, either. He might not care if West Anderson liked him dating his sister but he also wasn't one to run and tattle, either. At least Jason had been realistic about his baby sister and dating.

"I had some coffee and pie at the diner with your brother Jason. He's going to do some of the research on Drew and the attendees. Criminal records and the like."

A graceful brow arched in question. "Are you looking into my background?"

"You have an airtight alibi. Me. But I am interested in if you saw anything suspicious or out of the ordinary. Did anyone's behavior surprise you?"

Their entrees were placed in front of them and they both dug in unashamedly. The steak was cooked to perfection and his stomach was growling.

"Darrell and Troy were a surprise but then again, not really. They were both loose cannons back in high school and known for pushing the boundaries. Darrell always had a big mouth and

Troy was always in one scrape after another. What about you? Did you see anything you thought was strange?"

He liked that Leann wanted their conversations to be a back and forth. Zach had spent time with too many women who only wanted to hear the sound of their own voices.

"Nothing that stood out. No one appeared to be casing the joint or separating themselves from the crowd. That's what I was mainly looking for. I think this killer feels isolated and betrayed."

"By us?"

"You, his family, his friends, the world. I think this person has a victim complex. Whenever anything bad has happened to them it's always someone else's fault. Because of their self-delusion it would be difficult for them to have a true and close relationship. They'd have superficial friendships and romances but real intimacy would be a struggle." Zach laughed and took another bite of his steak. "I could be completely wrong, though. I'm still quite new at profiling."

"It makes sense from a psychological standpoint," Leann replied. "If a person feels like they're always the victim and never at fault that's going to impair their interpersonal relationships. I've actually seen this in my practice of marriage counseling. The couple looks and acts totally normal to the outside world. Usually the partner who feels they are a victim has managed to learn to mimic proper loving behavior, but eventually they come to resent having to act that way as they feel that their partner has received, and I quote, 'more than their share' of the love in the marriage. It's like they're keeping score in their lives. There's a great deal of the blame game in a relationship like that and often the other partner learns to simply take the blame to keep the peace."

Zach pulled out his phone and tapped a note into it. "I'm making a note of that. Keeping score in their lives. That's interesting. When I'm questioning suspects I can bend the conversation to see if that's how they feel. That's fantastic, Leann. You're a big help in this. Maybe you should be the profiler."

"Maybe Jason would give me a job," she laughed. "But I'm still impressed. For someone without a psychology background you seem to have a handle on behavioral analysis. Do you have any more hidden talents?"

He pretended to ponder her question, stroking his chin. "Not that I can think of. Oh wait…there is one other thing…I can touch the tip of my nose with my tongue."

Giggling, Leann covered her mouth with her napkin. "Evidence. I want evidence."

"Not here." Grinning, he looked around the restaurant. "Everybody will be jealous and wish they were me."

"I'm holding you to this. I have to see this feat of physicality."

"It's basically a stupid human trick, like a seal balancing a ball on its nose, but I appreciate the enthusiasm. I promise I'll show you sometime."

"I have one, too."

The fork paused halfway to Zach's lips. "Pardon?"

"I have a stupid human trick, too. You're not the only talented one sitting at this table, Zach."

He hadn't had this much fun on a date in ages. Maybe ever. Where had Leann been all these years?

It's not a date.

It could be. She's into me. I'm into her.

What about West?

Fuck him.

"Are you going to share?"

Straightening in her chair, she appeared inordinately proud of herself. "I can rub my stomach and pat my head at the same time. You can ask my brothers. They've seen me do it. None of them can, though."

No wonder she was proud of herself. It couldn't have been easy to grow up with all that testosterone in the house. It would have been shocking if she *hadn't* moved away after college. She'd needed a place to shine for herself and not for her family name.

"Will you show me?" Zach asked. "Not here, of course."

"I will. Prepare to be amazed."

The buzzing of his phone made him groan out loud. With an open murder case, he couldn't ignore it no matter how much he was enjoying himself tonight. It might be the crime lab or the medical examiner.

"I'm so sorry but I have to take this."

Nodding, she continued eating. "It's okay. I get that you have a lot going on."

The call was from the night shift supervisor.

"Gibson. What's going on, Ledell?"

Zach's heart sped up as he listened to the officer's news. There would be no time for chocolate mousse tonight.

"Thanks. I'll be right there." He gave Leann an apologetic look as he ended the call. "I'm not sure how much you heard but they've found Troy and brought him in for questioning."

"That is important but I'm sorry you'll miss the dessert." She looked at him from under her lashes. "Maybe another time?"

Was she hinting that she wanted to go out on another date? Hell, yes. West could kiss Zach's ass. Jason at least was supportive, and even if he wasn't, after tonight Zach wouldn't have cared.

"It's a promise," he replied, signaling the waiter for the check. "We can get that chocolate mousse to go. I'll drop you at Dizzy's while I'm questioning Wallace. I can have a deputy watch the house for a few hours."

"I can get a–"

Reaching across the table, he caught her hand, so small and delicate compared to his own.

"I'll drive you to Dizzy's where I know you'll be safe. Questioning Wallace won't take long. Then I'll come by to get you. You're still staying with me. If anyone wants to hurt you they're going to have to go through me."

"Let's hope that doesn't happen." She finished the last bite of her dinner. "I can't wait to hear what Troy has to say about where he's been since last night."

"You and me both, Leann."

Chapter Fifteen

LEANN HAD QUICKLY visited the ladies' room while Zach paid the check. She was sorry to see their evening end so early but the case had to come first and she understood that. He'd made it clear there would be other nights so it was all good.

Too bad there wouldn't be a kiss at the end of the evening.

Still no kiss. She was getting impatient but now at least she was hopeful. He wanted to kiss her too. She could feel it.

"Leann!"

She turned to see West's assistant Lori entering the restaurant with her husband Brad.

"Lori, it's so good to see you."

They hugged and Leann shook Brad's hand since she'd only met him a few times in the past.

"I knew you were back in Tremont," Lori smiled, her arm hooked with her husband's. "West mentioned it the other day. For the reunion, right?"

"Yes, it was last night."

The girl's smile dimmed. "I heard about Drew. Such a sad thing. Poor Jenna. I'm hoping to get by there tomorrow to pay my respects."

"I'm sure she'll be happy to see you. There was a full house today."

"I'll definitely go after church tomorrow." Lori's eyes lit up as she gazed over Leann's shoulder. "I see you're here with Zach. Looks like West didn't scare him off at all."

Say what?

"I'm not sure what you mean."

"West called Zach in early this morning. I couldn't hear every word that was said, of course." *Really? You're slipping, Lori.* "But West was warning him off, although Jason seemed fine with the two of you. Good for Zach that he didn't listen."

"Yes, good for Zach," Leann replied, already planning West's slow, agonizing death.

The hostess stood in front of them with an air of expectation.

"Oops, looks like our table is ready," Lori giggled. "Stop by the office and maybe we can go to lunch or something. I'd love a good long catch up."

"I will. Have a nice dinner."

Lori and Brad passed Zach as he joined her in the foyer of the restaurant. "Is that West's assistant?"

"It is," Leann confirmed. "I hear that you had a meeting with my brother this morning. Care to share any of those details?"

His smile grew wider, his cheeks turning a ruddy shade. "I think you already know all of the pertinent information. And the answer to your unspoken question is no. I was not planning on telling you, although I assumed you'd find out sooner or later—this being Tremont and all."

"You're going to have another murder to investigate because I'm going to kill West."

Leann was going to make her brother pay dearly for interfering in her life.

"I understand why he's upset you," Zach agreed, wrapping an arm around her waist and leading her to the door. "But I get why he's protective. You're his little sister. I feel the same way about Gigi and Aubrey."

"Did you threaten West or Travis?"

"No, but I could see that they were happy."

It was her turn to blush. "He doesn't get to decide if I'm happy or not."

Opening the car door for her, he reached for her arm before she could get in, his fingers skating across her elbow and sending a shiver up her spine. "Are you? Happy, I mean?"

The question was asking a hell of lot more than her emotional state and for a second it felt like her heart skipped a beat in her chest. This attraction that had been growing between them was having a moment…right now. She'd been wanting it and here it was.

Don't screw this up.

She smiled and squeezed his hand. "I am. Very happy. How about you?"

His smile showed off even white teeth and a dimple in one cheek. "I'm happy too, Leann."

"Tomorrow I'll deal with my brother," Leann sighed, plotting all sorts of bodily harm on her sibling. "I'm going to educate him. It will be painful."

Zach smirked. "Learning is never easy. I kind of feel sorry for the poor guy. If it makes you feel any better, your brother Jason specifically said he wasn't going to warn me off and that you were a smart woman who could make her own decisions."

"That makes one man in the Anderson family that's not an imbecile. The testosterone…it burns."

TROY WALLACE HADN'T come quietly from the looks of things. His eye was already turning purple and the corner of his lip was swollen. His clothes were dirty and his sleeve was ripped. He'd put up a good fight, that was for sure. Zach couldn't help but wonder what the officers who brought him in looked like.

The interrogation room was impersonal and stark on purpose with its puke green walls and bare furnishings – nothing but a table and two uncomfortable wooden chairs. Zach took the chair across from Troy and settled in for the long haul. His suspect didn't look like he was in the mood to be cooperative.

"Wallace, glad you could join us tonight."

"Fuck you."

It was one of the nicer things that had been said to Zach during questioning.

"Now are you aware that Drew Marshall was murdered last night at the reunion?"

Slumped in the chair, a sullen look on Troy's face, the man didn't look like he was going to answer the question so Zach was surprised when he replied.

"I heard." Terse and to the point. "What does that have to do with me?"

As if he didn't know. Surely Troy had watched enough cop

shows to know what was going on.

"You're a person of interest in this case. You were read your rights by the officer that brought you in. Would you like an attorney to be provided for you?"

That had Troy sitting up in his chair. "I don't have anything to hide. I didn't do anything wrong, man."

Good cop or bad cop? Zach decided on the former, based on nothing more than a gut feeling. The body language he was reading right now said this guy needed a friend. An enemy would simply make him clam up.

"I'm sure you didn't. I just want to hear your side of the story."

Troy's lips twisted and he huffed out a breath. "You want to hear my side of the story? I'll tell you my side. That little bitch Jenna led me on. One minute she's rubbing up against me and the next she's telling her husband that I'm hitting on her."

"You had a crush on her in high school," Zach said, keeping his tone as neutral as possible. If Troy felt like he was being judged he'd stop talking.

Shrugging, Troy shook his head.

"Sure, I liked her. So did a lot of guys. She wasn't as pure and angelic as she wanted everyone to believe. She screwed a bunch of guys." Troy grinned. "She and I fucked in the back of my old man's Chevy one night after a basketball game. Good old Drew was home with the flu. I doubt she ever told him about that, though."

Troy and Jenna? He didn't appear to be making anything up, his expression clear and direct. He'd made eye contact with Zach and his body position wasn't closed off. It could be, however, that Troy simply believed what he was saying. But that didn't make it true.

"So she was flirting with you last night?"

Troy slapped the table. "She damn well was and then had the nerve to act like it never happened. I wouldn't have gone after her without any encouragement. You know, her being married and all."

You're a real humanitarian.

"So after you and Drew fought where did you go?"

"I left," Troy emphasized the last word. "I got the hell out of there and headed down to Lucky's where they don't water down the drinks. I never wanted to go to that stupid reunion anyway."

And yet you did.

"Were there any witnesses?"

Troy smiled. "A whole bar full of them. I played pool and darts and left at closing time."

"I'll check on that. So where have you been all day? Did you know that the police wanted to talk to you?"

"I took a load of hay up to Sullivan and hung around. The cops pulled me over when I was coming home. Are we done?"

"For now. If your alibi doesn't check out we'll be having another discussion, though."

"I can't wait," jeered Troy, levering to his feet. "Listen, if you want someone that had a beef with Drew you need look no further than his good friend Darrell. They were…what do you call it? Frenemies. They competed for everything and poor old Darrell usually came out on the losing end. After awhile that has to piss a man off, you know what I mean?"

Darrell Madison? Based on what Wallace said, he just might fit the profile. But where was he?

Chapter Sixteen

AFTER ZACH DROPPED her off, Leann had the deputy drive her to West and Gigi's home a few miles away. He waited in the cruiser as she ran the doorbell, taking deep breaths and trying to rein in her rising temper. If she was going to move back – and it was shit like this that made her go back and forth about it – the first step was to put in place some boundaries between herself and her family. That started today. Right now. Unknowingly, West had opened up a huge issue and she was about to give him hell and then some for overstepping. Zach was the nicest man she'd met in a long time.

The door swung open and West stood there with a surprised look on his face. "Hey, little sister. We didn't expect to see you until tomorrow at dinner. Come on in." He peered out the door and saw the cop. "You brought a babysitter?"

"Thanks," she replied, following him into the living room where Gigi sat on the sofa feeding their baby son Ryder. "Zach is at the station questioning Troy Wallace."

"Leann, what a lovely surprise," Gigi gushed, smiling and waving to a comfortable chair. "Come sit down and visit a little while. When he's done feeding you can even hold Ryder if you want."

Now Leann felt a little silly. As pissed off as she was, she hadn't expected to walk in to this cozy domestic scene with Gigi feeding the baby and West…holy shit…was her brother doing dinner dishes? That was one for the books.

The words still needed to be said, however, and she was here so she might as well say them.

"I hear you had a little chat with Zach this morning. Want to tell me about that?"

Her brother had the good sense to look ashamed, his cheeks turning red as he sat down on the couch next to his wife. Perhaps he was hoping Gigi and the baby would protect him.

"I asked him to come in and talk about Drew Marshall's murder."

Settling into a chair opposite, Leann clutched her purse on her lap, her knuckles white with the anger she held bottled up inside. Yelling wasn't the answer here no matter how much she wanted to let fly.

"Did you talk about anything else?"

West's gaze dropped to the floor and he shifted uncomfortably on the couch as if he was being poked and prodded with a pointy stick.

"We might have chatted about other topics. Why do you ask?"

Leann stared at her brother, floored by his aversion to the truth. He was always spouting off about honesty and integrity but when it came to running her life he didn't give a shit.

"Do you lie to everyone in your life or just me? Does Gigi know you're a big fat liar? Does she know that you don't think her own brother is good enough for an Anderson?"

To Gigi's credit, she didn't get angry or upset. Instead her brow arched and she gave her husband a mean look. "For the love of all that's good and holy, what have you done now, Westin Anderson? Look at me."

Swallowing hard, West lifted his head and tried to look his wife in the eyes. "I was just worried."

Sighing, Gigi rolled her eyes. "You better start talking and fast or you are going to have not one but two women put their foot in your ass, then make you wear it as a hat."

Leann had never had an ally before in her battle with her nosy, overbearing brothers. This was nice.

"Your brother is interested in our Leann," he said defensively, his arms waving in the air to emphasize his point. "So I talked to him. Going after the little sister of a friend is completely against the bro-code."

Dear Lord in heaven, save them all from the dreaded bro-code.

"The nerve of him," Gigi exclaimed in mock horror. "A good, honest, hard working man like my brother Zach interested in a woman. What's next? The zombie apocalypse? If I didn't have my hands full I'd smack the back of your head. In fact, I may have Leann do it. It might knock a little sense into you."

Leann had been silent so far, letting Gigi take her husband to task, but this was her fight and she needed to do it herself.

"Did you hear yourself?" Leann asked her big brother, so pissed off that her voice shook. "Did you hear what you said? You called me 'our Leann' as if I don't belong to myself. As if I'm an object that you and everyone else own and only share when you feel like it. I'm a human being, West, with thoughts and opinions of my own. It's sad that after all these years you only see me as an extension of yourself."

"That's not true," he protested, his face becoming even redder. "I was just worried about you."

"Why?" she shot back immediately. "Why were you worried? What horrible fate did you think awaited me from dating Zach?"

Jumping up from the couch, West paced his living room. It appeared to Leann that he delaying long enough to come up with a palatable reason for his actions.

"I just didn't want you to get hurt. Is it a crime to worry about my baby sister? If it is, just lock me up and throw away the key."

West even tossed a pretend key into the air to emphasize his point.

"Don't be a drama king," Gigi said sharply, her narrowed-eyed gaze on West. "Your sister asked you a question and she deserves a serious answer. Do you have one? Because I'd like to hear it too."

West rounded on the two women and pointed to Leann. "I don't have to take this shit. Both of you ganging up on me. It isn't fair. I did what I did because I was worried about Leann. That's my right as her brother."

West stomped outside and Leann sat rooted to the spot, once again questioning the wisdom of moving home. She didn't want it to be like this but no one was too supportive of these boundaries she needed in place.

"He's exhausted and sleep-deprived," Gigi said, her tone apologetic. "Normally he'd be happy to argue with you all night long until every cow in the county was fast asleep. Now do you want to hold your nephew?"

"I certainly do. He's even cuter than the pictures you sent me."

The warm, sweet-smelling bundle was placed in Leann's arms and she dropped a kiss on Ryder's forehead. "Don't worry about me and your daddy. We always argue but we always make up. Everything is going to be fine."

"Yes, it will be."

West's voice swung her attention from the baby to where he was standing in the doorway of the kitchen, his shoulders stiff. He crossed his arms over his chest and lifted his chin. "I have something to say."

"Then you should say it."

"I'm not going to apologize for doing what I think is right. I was worried about you and so I gave him a little nudge. You should be thanking me that I care this much."

It was laughable. "You're doubling down on this strategy? I have to give you credit, brother dear—most people wouldn't stand behind their high-handed, asinine actions but you make it look like art. You must think I'm an idiot."

He shook his head. "I think you're an incredibly smart woman, Sis. Hell, a lot smarter than me."

"But still stupid."

He threw his hands in the air. "Why do you keep saying that?"

"Because you think I'm too dumb to know whether a man is good or bad. Whether he's the kind to cheat. You think I'm too stupid to make my own decisions despite evidence to the contrary. I've been doing that for many years, you know, and so far I haven't done too bad of a job. I'm tired of you acting as if I don't have a brain in my head because I'm a girl. I'm standing up and telling you right now that I simply will not allow you to interfere in my life any longer."

His face had gone red again. "I just thought–"

"Stop," she said firmly, standing to hand the baby back to Gigi. She was trembling too much to hold Ryder. Anger and a newborn didn't mix. "You seem to be under the impression that your opinion matters here. It does not. You don't get a vote on how I live my life, just as I don't get one about yours. What you think doesn't matter in the least. As in not at all. So you can stop this ridiculous behavior or you and I are going to be toe to toe constantly. But I warn you right now, I will not back down. You will keep your nose out of my affairs or I will do it for you. Have I made myself perfectly clear?"

"Crystal."

"Good." Leann turned to Gigi and tried to smile. "I'm sorry this wasn't a more pleasant visit. It was wonderful to see you and the baby. Hopefully we can do this again."

Gigi gave her husband some nasty side eye. Leann almost felt sorry for him because she had a feeling he was going to be sleeping on the couch tonight. "It's certainly not your fault. You're welcome here any time."

"Listen, this whole argument is for nothing. I talked to Jason after Zach left my office and I'm not going to interfere anymore," West said, rubbing the back of his neck. "I actually think that you and Zach would make a nice couple."

Gigi's eyes narrowed at her husband and Leann was more than suspicious as well. West didn't often change his stubborn, obstinate mind so easily.

"You talked to Jason about this?" Leann asked cautiously. "And what did he have to say that was so life-changing?"

"You know…that Zach was a good guy." West shifted on his feet. "That we should be happy that you two like each other. That kind of stuff."

That kind of stuff? What in the ever-loving hell?

"So he didn't say anything different than I did but because it came from a man it meant more? Is that what you're saying?"

"That's not it at all," West said loudly but then realized his baby son was in the room. "He just explained it in a different way."

Gigi's brows had shot up. "Wow, he must have made one hell of an argument. But let's get to the heart of the matter here. Are you going to stay out of Leann's love life and respect her decisions?"

"I am," West said firmly.

We'll see about that.

"And you're going to tell my brother that you're not opposed to him dating Leann?"

West shrugged. "Sure, I can do that."

"Tomorrow," Leann replied sharply. "You'll do it tomorrow at dinner."

She now understood why Zach had run so hot and cold these past few days. Gathering up her purse, she leaned down to kiss little Ryder on the forehead one more time.

"Since we seem to have come to an agreement, I'll head out so you two can get back to your evening. I'll see you tomorrow at dinner."

"We'll be there," Gigi said with a smile. "Ryder will probably sleep a little bit and you and I can catch up."

"Goodnight, brother dear."

"Always fun when you stop by, Leann," West mocked with his signature grin as he accompanied her to the door. "Let's do this more often."

If she moved back they just might. This wasn't the first time they'd gone five rounds and sadly it wouldn't be the last. He couldn't see that he was treating her like a child and she couldn't allow him to do it anymore. It had been easier to simply leave town and live somewhere else, but if she was going to move back here something had to be done.

Tonight had been the first step. Only about a million more to go.

Chapter Seventeen

THE ANDERSON RANCH was breathtakingly beautiful. It was also overwhelmingly large. Zach and Leann had been driving for twenty minutes after coming through the gate and could only now see the house in the distance. He had been out to the ranch many times but he could never get over the size of it. It was almost a little town unto itself.

When he parked the car, Leann didn't get out right away, instead turning toward him to speak. "I should probably tell you that I went over to West's last night while you were questioning Troy Wallace."

This was the first he was hearing about this. Accident? No way.

"You didn't mention this when I picked you up at Dizzy's last night. How did you even get there?"

"I asked the deputy guarding me to drive."

She was ballsy and resourceful. She had also been furious. Poor West.

"Do I dare guess what you discussed with our esteemed mayor?"

Leann smirked. "I think you know what the conversation

was about, although West said that Jason had spoken to him and that now he wasn't going to try and stand in our way."

Zach hadn't known Leann long but he couldn't imagine that statement going over well.

"What did you say, I ask with fear in my heart?"

"That his opinion didn't matter either way and that I was a grown woman who was going to do whatever I damn well pleased. He said he was trying to help. I told him not to bother. Even Gigi was mad at him."

Now *that* Zach could easily picture. West might like to swagger around but Gigi didn't put up with any of his shit.

"So you're telling me this is kind of a warning that your brother might not be very friendly today?"

She pushed open her car door and gave him a quick smile. "I just wanted to let you know that I handled this. If West acts like an ass today it will be because he is actually an ass."

The front door of the large house swung open and a welcoming David Anderson stood there with a wide grin, motioning for them to come in. Zach and Leann were not the first to arrive. Jason and West along with Gigi were already there. Travis and his wife Aubrey would be absent. They were out of town on a business trip and Brinley, Jason's wife, was home with a cold. She'd insisted Jason come anyway, probably so she could get some peace and quiet to rest.

The Anderson family came together for dinner but liked to separate by gender beforehand. Leann disappeared into the kitchen with the other females, leaving Zach facing a wall of Anderson men. Normally that didn't bother Zach but then he'd never been in this position. Luckily, they all seemed friendly today, even West. Zach had always got on well with the Anderson family.

David was playing bartender and poured everyone a shot of whisky. No way was Zach turning it down. He could use a drink.

“So how is the murder case going?” David asked, holding up a cigar in offering. Was this a test? Zach couldn’t imagine Leann liked the scent of a smelly cigar on a man. Honestly, he wasn’t too fond of it either.

“No, thanks. I don’t smoke.”

Laughing, Jason shook his head at his father. “We don’t smoke them. Not really. Mostly Dad does it to rile up Mom every now and then.”

West held out his hand. “I’ll take one.”

The women must have wolf-like hearing because Gigi stuck her head out of the kitchen. “Don’t you dare, Westin Anderson. I won’t have you smoking that in the same house as our child. Do you want to sleep in the garage?”

“She said your whole name,” Jason mocked his brother. “You’re in big trouble.”

West shrugged like he didn’t care. “Haven’t you heard? I already am. I had to sleep on the couch last night. Leann came over and Gigi found out about our conversation with Zach. They both threatened to make me wear my ass as a hat.”

David Anderson chuckled as he sat down in a big brown leather chair. “That’ll mess up your hair, son. Maybe you should think about staying out of your adult sister’s life. It might save your own.”

Now this was fascinating. Watching the father handle the

son. Zach kept his mouth shut wondering what might be said or done next.

West out his hands up in surrender. "I am staying out of it. In fact, I am now Leann and Zach's biggest cheerleaders."

That was just plain weird. It was one thing for Jason and West to not interfere in Leann's love life but to actively root for them as a couple? Strange as hell.

Jason chuckled. "That would be a change because we made her teenage years a nightmare when it came to boys, practically running them off before they even got to the door. Just like you did yesterday to Zach. Except Leann and Zach are two consenting adults who don't give a shit what you think."

"Actually, I care even less than that."

Leann's voice. She didn't sound angry at her brothers, more tired than anything else. Zach guessed that she'd been worn down by these males on too many occasions to count.

"Drink, sweetheart?" her father asked.

"Martini, please." Leann swung her attention from her father back to Jason. "From what I've seen you're the only Anderson male that has a lick a sense."

David cleared his throat loudly. "I heard that."

The door to the kitchen flew open and Gigi and Eileen Anderson walked into the living room. Gigi was giving her husband a look that Zach wouldn't ever want to see from a woman and West didn't appear to like it. The back of his neck was now a ruddy shade and he couldn't meet his wife's gaze.

"I'm guessing Leann meant for you to hear that, dear," Eileen replied to her husband. "You don't come out of this situation squeaky clean either, so let's not pretend you do."

"I was only trying to protect my teenage daughter. I have nothing to apologize for."

Eileen handed Leann one of the martini glasses. "You keep telling yourself that and perhaps you'll start believing it."

"Am I allowed to ask Zach about the murder investigation?" West asked. "Since I've repented and given up my bossy ways?"

"Actually, I'd like to hear about that too," Leann replied eagerly. "You left dinner last night to question Troy Wallace. Did you learn anything useful?"

Just like that, West and Leann weren't mad anymore. This Anderson family was going to give Zach whiplash the way they turned on a dime.

He knocked back the rest of his whiskey. "I'm not even sure where to start."

✦ ✦ ✦

THE ENTIRE FAMILY was settled at the table for dinner and the food smelled delicious. Little Ryder had fallen back asleep and was sleeping in his bassinet in the living room. Sneaking a quick look at Zach, Leann could only wonder what he thought about all of this.

This wasn't his first Sunday dinner with the Anderson family but it had to be far different than what he'd grown up with. The long table was filled with people and food, all speaking loudly to be heard over one another. As much as Zach longed to create a family for himself the question remained... Is that what he'd had in mind? Or something quiet and calm?

Once everyone's plate was full the table quieted down and everyone was ready to hear more details from Zach's investigation. He'd already discussed how they were still looking for Darrell and trying to account for everyone's whereabouts at the time of the murder.

"I spoke with Troy Wallace last night as you know." Zach gave Leann an apologetic look. "He swears that Jenna was flirting with him and then she ran to Drew to tell him that Wallace was hitting on her. He also swears that they had...a thing...back in high school."

Everyone was looking at Leann for some sort of verification. "I...well...I don't know. I don't remember them ever hooking up but it could have happened, I suppose."

Troy and Jenna? It was possible. Despite how Jenna acted, she hadn't been innocent in high school while Drew played the field. Both of them had run a little wild at times and a tryst with Troy wasn't something Jenna would want anyone to know. Even Leann.

Zach shrugged. "He can't prove it and honestly it's not important either way what happened one night fifteen years ago. What's important is the veracity of his statement of Friday night's events. I was able to verify his alibi with the folks down at Lucky's so I think he's out as a suspect."

"Then we're down to just Darrell Madison?" West asked. "He can't hide out forever. He's not that bright."

"Jared is also looking into the backgrounds of the victims. We might find another suspect there that connects all of them," Jason said. "But the most important thing right now is to keep Leann safe. These people are from her social circle. She could be next."

She still couldn't believe that anyone wanted her dead. "I

don't know what I would have done to deserve being killed, but then I don't know that Carole, Bitty, or Drew did anything either. This whole situation just feels so strange."

"Perhaps you should move out here to the ranch, baby girl," her father suggested. "Where we can keep an eye on you."

Leann opened her mouth to object but to her amazement Jason beat her to it. "Zach has all of this under control, Dad. He's guarding her twenty-four-seven."

David smiled at Zach. "I have no doubt you're doing a fine job, son, but it might be easier to guard her here. There's not as many people around."

"But the ranch is too remote," Jason argued. "If we needed the cops or, heaven forbid, an ambulance it would take way too long for them to get here. Plus, there's a hell of a lot of empty country surrounding us. The killer could sneak up from just about any direction. At least in town he has limited options. If I were the killer I'd want Leann out here. Less people to see me get in and out and less people to hear me. At least in town there are neighbors and traffic cameras. Plus, Zach's home has an excellent security system."

Leann and Zach exchanged puzzled glances. Jason was certainly pushing back against their father about this.

"But we could give Zach a break now and then." David wasn't going to back down on this. "Is the poor boy supposed to stay awake and never sleep?"

"We've got that handled," Jason persisted. "A few of the deputies give him a break when he needs it and at night they're patrolling his neighborhood."

Leann's father appeared dubious but West piped up as well.

"Leann should definitely stay with Zach. It's the safest place for her."

Giving her a funny look, Zach finally spoke up for himself. "I appreciate the vote of confidence but if you all think Leann would be safer here I understand."

"What do you think?" Elaine asked, her case darting from son to son and then back to Zach. "You're the one with experience protecting celebrities."

From the sour look on Jason's face he didn't think much of his own mother discounting his years in the DEA.

"I think," Zach began carefully, watching the expressions around the table, "that the killer would love to have Leann in a remote location. Remember that's exactly what suspects do when they kidnap a victim. They take them someplace where they can be alone and no one's around. There are plenty of places like that not far from your front door, Elaine. At least in town he has to work a little harder, plus Jason makes a good point. Assistance is much closer. However, if Leann feels safer out here then I can set up her security at the ranch. It can be done and I have no problem doing that. We can make it work."

Leann rolled her eyes. "Finally someone who is asking what I want."

Her father cleared his throat. "I'm just looking out for you, sweetheart."

"I know, Dad, and I love you but if Jason, West, and Zach all agree that the best place for me is to be in town then I think that's where I should be. Honestly, I'm simply trying not to be a burden while they're trying to catch a killer. Whatever is easier for them is what I want."

Jason slapped the table and grinned. "Then it's settled. Leann stays with Zach. Mom, is there dessert?"

Gigi was giving both Jason and her husband a strange look but she didn't speak up, instead focusing on her mashed potatoes. She did, however, give Leann a wink before elbowing West when he refilled his plate for a third time.

Sunday dinner at the Anderson's was never boring and today was no exception. Jason and West were acting…different. Leann couldn't put her finger on it but something was *off* with those two. While Zach was finding a murderer she was going to figure out just what her siblings were up to.

If there was trouble anywhere, Jason and West would find it.

Chapter Eighteen

THERE WERE MANY traditions in the Anderson household and one of Leann's favorites was that if the women did the cooking then the men did the cleaning. Since Zach was a guest he was excused from dish duty but her brothers and father grumbled good-naturedly all the way from the table to the kitchen.

Jason had suggested that Leann take Zach out to the gazebo to get some fresh air which she thought was…strange. Again. Something was definitely going on. Everyone in the family knew the gazebo was for kissing. Ever since the Anderson kids had hit puberty, their dates had been taken out to the gazebo for hand holding and some innocent necking. Not anything more, though, because it could be seen from the back windows of the house. Not well, but enough that no one was going to do anything scandalous there.

Leann had to admit that it was a romantic spot. Years of careful tending by Elaine had the flowers and greenery circling the structure and climbing the lattice and columns. The gazebo sat next to the lake and she had many wonderful memories of summer days, swimming, and picnics. In all her travels over the years, there was something about the ranch that she hadn't been able to find anywhere else in the world. The sweet smell of the grass, the wide open spaces. It all called to her even when she was far away.

"This is my favorite place," she said as they walked closer to the serene water. The sun beat down but the trees gave them welcomed shade. "On really hot days we used to come down here and cool off. I swear nothing felt better than plunging straight in after working all day outside."

Kneeling down, Zach dipped his hand in the water, then quickly pulled it out. "Damn, that is cold, woman. That's a little past refreshing and well on its way to hypothermia. Have you lost your marbles?"

Laughing, she settled under the shade of the gazebo on one of the benches. "I didn't say that we stayed in it very long, just that it felt good."

Standing, he shook the water from his arm and then climbed the gazebo steps to sit next to her. "So is it just me or are Jason and West acting weird?"

Slapping her forehead, Leann groaned in frustration. "You noticed it too? I thought maybe it was just me. Those two are definitely up to something and I'm determined to figure out what it is. They're not smart enough to keep it hidden for long."

"Wait a minute, wasn't Jason undercover for years infiltrating drug cartels?" Zach asked with a chuckle. "I think he might know a thing or two about covert operations."

"Those drug lords weren't his sister. I can smell the subterfuge on them. This is exactly like the time they wanted to throw a party when Mom and Dad were going to be out of town but they had to be careful so my aunt and uncle didn't find out. Which if you think about it is hilarious, because the whole town was going to know eventually and then my parents would know. But Jason and West were determined to try to do it and so they started planning in secret, keeping it from me and Travis. I'm sure you know how this turned out."

"Your parents found out."

"Everyone knew but Jason and West were bound and determined to have this party. Of course, they got caught and grounded for life, or something close to it. Travis and I just laughed at them all that summer because they were on restriction and could barely leave the ranch. We had all the fun and they were given all the crappy chores. And believe me, there are a ton of crappy jobs on a ranch."

"I'm not used to seeing Jason through your eyes. I see him as my super-smart employer who knows the ins and outs of investigation and surveillance. The way you talk about him he could be a Keystone cop."

Leann shrugged. "He is super smart and cool but he is not perfect. Not by a long shot. It's a sister's job to remind her swaggering, alpha male brothers just how imperfect they are."

"I've been taken down a peg or two by Gigi and Aubrey," Zach confessed. "They keep me humble."

"It goes both ways. They never let me get too enamored of myself, always making fun of the way I looked—especially my hair."

His fingers skated down a few strands, barely touching them. She couldn't even feel it, not really, but simply watching him do it sent a bolt of electricity through her body.

"I think your hair is amazing. Gorgeous and like silk."

An onlooker could probably hear the crackle of awareness between them. They'd been interrupted last night but this was their second chance. Not wanting it to pass them by, Leann lifted her face so she was looking up into Zach's blue eyes only to find him gazing at her with a tender expression. They were both thinking the same thing.

She had to remind herself to breathe. "So…"

Smiling, he slid his arm around her waist, pulling her closer to his much larger frame.

"So…"

Bending his head, he brushed his lips against hers. Once. Twice. Three times before deepening the kiss. Her arms creeped around his neck and his fingers tangled in her hair as his tongue swirled around hers. When they finally broke the kiss she was dizzy and breathless, her face and chest flushed. She would have been self-conscious but he too looked just as aroused, his eyes heavy-lidded and his shoulders rising and falling rapidly with his ragged breathing.

"That was…good," she panted, their gazes locked together. His normally soft blue eyes were dark, the pupils blown wide, and this time she didn't resist the urge to trace his jawline and the rough stubble underneath her fingertips.

"Very good," Zach agreed, a smile playing around his well-shaped mouth. "But I think we should do it again. You know, just to make sure."

One could never be too thorough.

✦ ✦ ✦

BACK AT ZACH'S home after dinner, Leann changed into sweats and a t-shirt while he checked his email. Dinner with her family had been rather exhausting, between trying to figure out what Jason and West were up to and also wanting to make a good impression on Leann's parents. Zach had spent time with David and Eileen in the past, of course, but now that he was involved with their daughter it was a whole new ballgame.

And he was involved with Leann. The kiss had sealed the deal. He didn't care what her brothers thought about the relationship.

Opening his laptop, Zach had several emails but the most important was from Jason Anderson's partner Jared – a preliminary report on Drew Marshall, although there was more to come according to the email. Jared described this report as "The stuff a little digging would find". Now he was going to work on uncovering "The stuff buried deep that no one wants you to know".

Leann joined him in the kitchen, settling into the chair opposite him at the table.

"Anything interesting?"

"Background on Drew Marshall."

"Are you still hoping to find a connection other than being classmates?"

Zach rubbed his chin, which was scruffy at the end of the day. "These people were killed with a lot of hate. Carole was bludgeoned to death. Bitty was strangled. Drew had his throat slit with a champagne bottle. These were not random murders and I'd bet my favorite pair of blue jeans that the killer knew Drew Marshall. Killing someone with a broken champagne bottle is too up close and personal. He had to face Drew and look him in the eye. That's an intense moment and nothing accidental about it."

Leann shuddered, her lips turning down. "Can you imagine facing a person that's trying to kill you? Basically seeing your own death? It's horrifying."

Zach opened the attachment on the email. "I think whomever killed Drew had a lot of hate for him. That's why this research is so important. It might give us a clue as to who would want him to die a painful death."

Peering over Zach's shoulder, Leann frowned. "You mean like his friends and enemies?"

"That and everything else we can get our hands on. Business partners. Finances. Group associations such as club memberships. Any lawsuits or arrests. Also family issues such as friction between himself and a sibling. Or his wife."

He'd casually dropped that last part, not sure how Leann would respond. Jenna was her friend and as such he assumed Leann would defend her.

"You want to find out if Jenna and Drew were having any marital difficulties?"

Scrolling through the report, he didn't see anything that jumped out at him. "Yes, it's standard operating procedure to investigate the spouse. Statistically, they should be our number one suspect."

"Is she?" Leann gave him a searching look. "Your number one suspect?"

"No, she's not. So far I don't have any evidence that points to Jenna but I would be remiss in my duties to exclude her from the investigation."

Blowing out a breath, Leann smiled. “I’m glad she’s not on your radar. I haven’t seen or talked to Jenna much these last fifteen years but she was always a good person. A little self-absorbed but I never saw her physically harm anyone. So do you see anything?”

“He and Jenna took a second mortgage on the house and they have quite a bit of credit card debt. He wasn’t ready for the poor house or anything but he wasn’t making much more than the minimum payments.”

“That doesn’t sound all that unusual.”

Zach scrolled farther down. “It’s not. It doesn’t look like he had any out of control spending, either. I don’t see any luxury purchases like jewelry, travel, or cars. What I do see is a man that is house rich and cash poor. It appears that he sunk every dime he had into that home and then some.”

Leann’s brows went up. “And that means…?”

“That he’s a normal middle-class American. So far, there’s nothing to write home about in this report. Drew Marshall was a typical average guy.”

✦ ✦ ✦

ZACH’S ASSESSMENT OF Drew’s life was fascinating. Just what was average these days?

“Typical?” Leann asked. “Can you elaborate?”

“From what this tells me, he went to work every day and came home to his wife and two kids. They have a dog and cat and a minivan. His kids are involved in sports and musical instrument lessons. They get decent grades but are no Einsteins. Jenna does volunteer work at her kids’ schools and goes to lunch once a week with her friends. She has two cocktails and a chicken Caesar salad normally. We can tell that detail from her credit card receipts. She has an addiction to reading police procedural novels. Drew liked political thrillers but reads much less. They had a Netflix subscription. Once a month they went out – probably a date night for the two of them – and had dinner at an upscale restaurant. He bought her flowers and candy on Valentine's Day. Jenna's Facebook feed is filled with puppies and kittens. Drew didn't have any social media accounts so I'm guessing he preferred face to face contact."

Leann pulled his laptop closer. "You can tell all of that? Holy shit."

"And more." Leann was horrified. Secrets were becoming extinct. "This is just the beginning. Jared will be able to dig much more deeply but it will take more time and effort. Do you have any secrets that you don't want the world to know?"

"No, and thank goodness because I bet you were about to tell me that it's too damn late. It's already out there."

"It is," he confirmed. "By the time we're done with Drew Marshall and his family – and the other victims as well – I'll know where every dime of his money went in the last five years. I'll know how often he took in his car for an oil change. I'll know what brand of beer was his favorite and I'll definitely know his favorite television show. All we have to do is follow his web footprint. In addition, we'll also interview some of the people on the edges of his life. His family and friends will try to cover up anything embarrassing. Coworkers or employees? The guy down at the Quickee Mart who sells him his coffee and gas? The kid that mows the lawn? They're happy to tell us every little detail, good or bad."

She couldn't help but feel sorry for Jenna, her family, and the relatives of Carole and Bitty. It was as if they were being victimized a second time. "That's a terrible invasion of privacy. Don't you feel a little guilty about ripping apart someone's life like this?"

Leann hadn't meant it to come out sounding so accusatory but luckily Zach didn't seem to take offense. "It sounds callous but if you're involved in a murder case your life is going to be inspected under a microscope. I do always apologize later but I have to do my job, Leann. I owe it to the victims."

"I know," she sighed, pushing her long hair back from her face. "It's just I hate to think of Jenna and the kids having to go through any of this."

Capturing a stray strand of hair between his fingers he tucked it behind her ear, his fingertips caressing her cheek and sending streaks of warmth straight to her abdomen. "I'll be as respectful as I can."

He would be, she was sure of it. She hadn't known him long but he had that air about him. Truth, honesty, and integrity. Her gut said she could trust this man no matter what. He reminded her of the men in her own family. They might not be perfect but they always tried to do the right thing.

She closed her eyes in contentment. "I know that too."

To her surprise and delight, Zach's nose nuzzled hers and his lips skated across her cheekbone, ever so lightly, sending a shiver up her spine. "How about we put the case away for the night?"

Her fingertips glided down his arm and over his palm where his larger hand trapped her much smaller one. "I think that's a good idea. What do you want to do instead?"

His wolfish grin was the answer she'd craved. "I was hoping to kiss you again. Any objections?"

None at all.

Chapter Nineteen

ZACH WAS IN a particularly good mood the next morning. He probably shouldn't be this happy since he still hadn't found the killer plaguing Leann's reunion but he couldn't seem to stop smiling.

Because of Leann.

Yesterday he'd decided to pursue a relationship with her no matter how her brothers felt about it. If their kisses had been anything to go by, she was certainly as attracted to him as he was to her. After coming back to his place last night, they'd spent a long time on the couch sipping wine and talking about every little thing they could in between kisses. Childhood, careers, friends, enemies, politics, religion, music, and movies. They had more than he'd imagined in common but there were differences too. Enough to make it interesting. He wouldn't be dating a carbon copy of himself, that was for sure. She was stubborn, opinionated, and wickedly smart. Basically? She was an Anderson.

A fact that had kept him up far past when they'd both gone to bed. It didn't bother him that their romance would be watched closely by not only her family but by almost everyone in town. He'd just ignore them all. What bugged him was the about-face Leann's brothers had taken when it came to her love life. Zach would have liked to think it was because it was him. They knew he wouldn't do anything to hurt their sister, but about three in the morning he'd woken up out of a sound sleep and sat straight up in bed. An idea had come into his head and once there he couldn't shake it. Jason and West were up to something and Zach was pretty sure he knew what it was.

Those Anderson boys thought they were so smart.

Leann shuffled into the kitchen, yawning and stretching. In just a few short days he'd learned that she wasn't a morning person. He already had the coffee and breakfast made.

"Sorry, I overslept," she said as she poured her first cup of the day. He'd also learned she didn't perk up until her second coffee. "Are we going to the office this morning?"

She'd agreed to shadow him today so he could still work and protect her at the same time. Hopefully she wouldn't be too bored. Investigation work wasn't always that exciting.

"We are but after we eat." He filled her plate with eggs, bacon, and toast. "How about I cook some steaks on the grill tonight? It's supposed to stay warm today."

She dug into her food with enthusiasm. "That sounds fantastic. I love your cooking but I feel a little guilty. I should be helping more."

Sitting down opposite her, he shrugged. "I like doing it so it's no big deal. I'll make a deal with you. If I get tired of cooking I'll let you know. You can either do it or we can eat out."

"Deal," she grinned, humming in appreciation at his scrambled eggs. "Damn, these are good."

"I didn't do anything special to them other than use some cheese."

"They taste better when they're not burnt."

From what Zach could tell, Leann didn't like to cook. Or she wasn't good at it. Or both.

They chatted about innocuous subjects while they ate – the weather, their plans for the day, but eventually Leann finished her second cup of coffee. It was time to talk to her about what he'd been up thinking about last night.

"I've been thinking," he began cautiously, not sure how she'd react to his theory.

"Is that dangerous?" she teased, taking their plates to the sink and rinsing them off.

"It might be. I was thinking about how your brothers suddenly are all on our side about dating. It just seemed…strange to me."

Wiping her hands on a dish towel, Leann nodded in agreement. "It does and it kind of worries me. What are they up to?"

"I have a theory," he confessed. "Jason was adamant about my protecting you twenty-four-seven almost from the beginning. Then all of the sudden your brother West is cheering for us? There's more to it than they think I'm a great guy. I think they're pushing us together to try and lure you back home, Leann."

She didn't look shocked or angry. Instead she sighed heavily and rolled her eyes. "I admit the thought crossed my mind as well. It would be just like them to try and manipulate me into coming home."

"You haven't said anything to them? That you're thinking

about moving back?"

"Give 'em an inch, they'll think they're a ruler," Leann groaned. "If I told them I was thinking about coming back they'd freak out and do something crazy. Well, crazier than trying to make us a couple. It's a creative solution to what they consider a problem. I wonder which one of them came up with it?"

"I think it was Jason."

"I think you're right. This little plan has his fingerprints all over it. West would have done something more overt. Jason is the subtle one."

Zach wasn't sure just how *subtle* this was but he'd bow to her judgment when it came to her own family. "The question is what do you want to do about it? Just ignore it? Call them on it?"

Her smile widened and her brown eyes sparkled as she waggled her eyebrows. "Do you want to have some fun with them?"

This. This right here was why Zach was so damn attracted to this woman.

"Hell yes, I do. What do you have in mind?"

ZACH AND LEANN'S evil plan for world domination was set by the time they reached his office. She headed off to torture her brother Jason while Zach stopped off at the admin assistant's desk to see if the forensics had come in from the state crime lab.

"Morning, Tina. Anything for me?"

Pushing her glasses up her nose, she nodded absently. "I printed it all off and set it on your desk." She finally looked up and smirked. "You should thank me, by the way. The mayor's assistant called me this morning asking if we'd heard anything from the state crime lab and I said no. Thought you might not want West Anderson sticking his nose into your investigation."

Inwardly chuckling, Zach wished he were shocked. West just couldn't seem to let go of police work. "Thank you, Tina. You're a treasure. As soon as I read through the report, I'll call West. I don't want to get you into trouble."

Zach had his own office and he shut his door and sat down, impatiently skimming through the paperwork Tina had left on his desk. The news was good. The lab was able to pull four prints off of the champagne bottle. Drew. Darrell. Colin. Nicole.

The first two Zach had expected but the second two were a surprise. How had Colin Simpson and Nicole Quincy managed to get their fingerprints on the bottle? It would be one of the first questions he asked both of them.

As for the rest of the report, there was confetti on the broken edge of the bottle and in the wound on Marshall's neck. The confetti matched the type used at the reunion. No surprise there either. Blood samples had been collected at the scene but DNA was going to take several more days. It wasn't like on television where results were given in hours. In reality, it was more like weeks.

The rope marks on Bitty's neck didn't have any evidence that could help them and the fingerprints on Carole's car hadn't come up with anything either. Zach was going to have to break this case another way because it didn't look like the science was going to help him at all. He needed to talk to Colin and Nicole. Somehow all these people were connected. It was more than the reunion; he felt it in his gut. What was he missing?

But there had been *four* sets of prints on that bottle and they had yet to talk to Darrell. He had motive, opportunity, and ability. Now he had a connection to the murder weapon. Plus he hadn't stepped forward to clear his name.

Where in the hell was Darrell Madison hiding?

✦ ✦ ✦

"I BROUGHT YOU some coffee, big brother. Say thank you."

Jason smiled and pointed to the guest chair in his office. "Thanks, little sis. I was ready for another cup. Are you here with Zach today?"

She placed the coffee in front of him but she didn't sit down, instead walking around the desk and looking out of the large window behind him. Jason had a lovely view of the park across the street but he chose to turn his back on it every day.

"Where else would I be? I'm in danger, after all."

"Why do I get the feeling that you don't believe you're in danger?"

She didn't, actually, and even if she did she was certain Zach could handle whatever or whoever wanted to hurt her.

"I guess I don't think anyone wants to kill me. Yes, Bitty, Carole, and Drew were part of my social circle in high school but so were a lot of people. Besides, the reunion is over now and we haven't had a dead body since Saturday night. Maybe the killer is done."

Jason sat back in his big leather chair, a contemplative look on his face. "That's certainly possible. Or it could be that they can't get to you and are waiting until we're more relaxed and our guard is down. I don't want that to happen."

"I can't have a bodyguard for the rest of my life. There are other people they could be targeting too. Jenna, Nicole, Troy, Henry, Sam. Should they all start traveling with an entourage to keep them safe?"

"I'm not going to let anything happen to you."

"Neither am I." Time to put plan their into action. "And I know Zach won't let anyone harm me. He's so protective."

Jason grinned, probably thinking he was a genius. "That's great to hear. I know I can trust him to keep you alive no matter what."

"It's wonderful that you're on our side so I know you'll be supportive."

His smile grew even wider. "I'm always on your side, Leann. If you and Zach want to date, fall in love, get married that's just fine with me."

Laughing, she shook her head. "I'm not sure we're ready to talk marriage at this point but I'm thrilled that he's open to the possibility of moving to Florida. In fact, he's kind of excited about it."

Jason blinked. Once. Twice. Three times as his smile seemed to fade.

"Move? What did you say? I mean…move? Zach's talking about moving?"

Leann felt kind of sorry for her brother at the moment, but then she reminded herself that he'd been trying to run her life. As usual.

"Obviously it's too early in our relationship to be making those kinds of decisions but if things keep going on the way that they are…" She smiled and sighed happily. "He's open to the idea, which is such a relief. I didn't want to get serious about someone that lived three thousand miles away."

Jason was staring at her blankly. "Three thousand miles…"

"And this is going to benefit you too." In for a penny, in for a pound. "Of course Zach will continue to travel for you as much as he does now but you can expand your consulting business to that part of the country so easily because he'll be living there. With me. Everybody wins."

Her big brother seem to wake up, frowning and rubbing his chin. "Everybody wins. Sure. That's great. This is all…great."

"And I have you to thank for it," Leann said, a smug smile on her face. The Anderson siblings were hard on one another but it was a tough love. Jason and West needed to learn to stay out of her life. "You're the one that put him in charge of my protection so we've spent all of our time together. If you hadn't done that, I doubt he and I would be where we are now."

Jason's throat worked as he swallowed hard. "I'm just glad I could help."

She reached across the desk and patted his hand. "You've done more than you could ever imagine."

Leann wouldn't let this go on forever. Just a few days. They needed to sweat and worry a little. But in the meantime she could only wonder how they would respond. No way would her brothers take this lying down and just give up.

Chapter Twenty

SOME DAYS WERE more productive than others and this one was shaping up to be a complete waste of time. In the morning, Zach had questioned Nicole Quincy about why her fingerprints were on the murder weapon and now he had to speak with Colin Simpson for the same conversation.

Nicole's answers had been short and to the point. She'd been on the committee that helped organize the reunion and had assisted a group of people unloading the booze after it had been delivered. She swore her fingerprints would be on many other bottles as well. As for her alibi, her husband vouched for her saying she was at home with him. Zach had never put much stock into spousal alibis but he'd definitely felt the "innocent" vibe from Nicole. No matter what Jenna said, he didn't think Nicole had any motive. She looked happy and content in her own life and her husband appeared to adore her. Zach had seen women trolling for their next husbands and Nicole didn't display that sort of behavior.

Colin, on the other hand, was not on the reunion committee so his prints were going to be harder to explain. Zach wasn't ready to call Colin a suspect yet. Darrell's prints had been on that bottle too, and he was still missing.

Simpson sat across from Zach in the conference room, unsmiling. "I can't believe you've asked me here. I had no reason to kill those people."

That wasn't entirely true. Colin Simpson had been picked on in high school by Drew Marshall, although that didn't explain Bitty and Carole. Instead of debating motive Zach went straight to the heart of why they were sitting there.

"Your fingerprints were found on the champagne bottle that killed Drew Marshall. I need to know how they got there."

"Simple." Colin shrugged, his body language as relaxed as someone's could be while being questioned. "After Darrell left I went to make a phone call and saw him out in the hallway when I was heading back to the party. He apologized and we shared a drink of champagne as a sign of peace between us. He drank straight from the bottle and so did I. That's why my fingerprints are there. I guess my DNA will be there too."

"What time was that?"

"I have no idea but I can check my phone's call log. I called my girlfriend right before I saw Darrell."

Technology was sometimes a good thing. "Let's see it."

Colin pulled the phone from his jacket pocket and scrolled to a spot in the call log before handing it to Zach. "Twelve-thirteen."

Drew's estimated time of death was between twelve-thirty and one. That put the murder weapon in Darrell's hands right before the incident.

"What did Darrell do after you shared a drink?"

"He was flirting with the girl at the front desk. I went back into the party."

"Did you see him again?"

Colin shook his head. "No, I left about thirty minutes later. Are we done here?"

"Can anyone corroborate your story?"

"Jesus, you're not kidding?" Colin looked thoroughly disgusted with the entire process. "That girl from the front desk saw me go back into the party. You can talk to her."

Zach would have to. It was part of the job.

"I will, thank you. If I have any more questions I'll be in touch."

The legs of the chair scraped against the tile as Colin pushed it back and stood. "I'm going home at the end of the week whether you like it or not. I didn't hurt anyone."

"I appreciate your cooperation, Mr. Simpson. Thank you for coming in today."

Colin stood but paused when he opened the door.

"If you want Drew's killer, you need to find Darrell and leave the rest of us alone. He had that champagne bottle."

"I'm trying to find him but it would seem he doesn't want to be found."

Colin smiled but it didn't reach his eyes. "Then you have your answer right there."

✦ ✦ ✦

ZACH GRILLED A mean steak. Tender, juicy, and just cooked to medium. To go with it he'd prepared scalloped potatoes and asparagus, and for dessert he'd picked up a chocolate cake at the local bakery. Every single bite of dinner was incredibly delicious.

After helping clear the table, he shooed Leann out on the back patio with a glass of wine.

"Relax and enjoy the nice weather. I'll join you in a minute. I just need to rinse these dishes."

"I could help," she offered again but it was mostly half-hearted. He wasn't going to let her and the evening really was lovely. She settled onto the glider and sipped her wine, letting the peacefulness of nature wash over her.

She could get used to this. Dinner and conversation with Zach, sharing their thoughts about the day. Intelligent and funny, he challenged her without being overbearing and he made her laugh without acting like a clown. There were so many wonderful things about him.

That was worrying. If he was truly this perfect he was going to get tired of her darn quick. She had a plethora of faults – some she was aware and probably many more she didn't.

He joined her after the dishes were done, sitting close with his arm around her shoulders. The night air caressed her skin but it was his fingers trailing lightly up her arm that raised goose-bumps.

"So what's wrong with you?"

Awesome. Wonderful. I've taken blurting to a whole new level.

"Um…lots of things," he chuckled as she buried her face in her hands. "I'm not sure where you're going here, Leann."

Fidgeting in her seat, she still couldn't make eye contact with him. She was mortified.

"It's just…you're so perfect. You're mature, understanding, a good cook. Heck, you even kiss well. There has to be something deeply wrong with you or you would be married by now. Why are you single?"

Chuckling warmly, he asked his own question. "Why are you single?"

It was a fair question, although she hadn't given it much thought. She'd been concentrating on what was wrong with the men in her life, not why she hadn't been ready to settle down.

"I haven't met the right man yet, plus I was very involved building my career. But if I'd met the right man, I would have made time for him."

Still smiling with amusement, Zach shrugged. "That's my explanation too. Meeting the right person plus timing. But in answer to your question, I have many faults. I can give you some names of my ex-girlfriends and they'd be happy to list them for you. Mostly they'd tell you I'm a workaholic that was commitment shy."

She could have applied that description to herself. Seems like they were two peas in a pod but where did that leave them? If she'd had a brain in her head she would have taken his explanation and just dropped the entire subject. But no…she was a glutton for punishment. They were already well down the rabbit hole so why not go for broke? It was better to know now than later.

"Do you not want to get married?"

Stroking his chin, he pondered her question before answering. "I do, but I haven't been in a hurry to get there. I was engaged once but it didn't work out."

Leann almost choked on her wine. That was a big detail he'd just revealed.

"Engaged? What happened?"

"She wanted to marry someone more conventional, someone who left the house in the morning for his commute and came home in time for dinner. That wasn't me at all. At the time I was doing personal security for a big movie star and would be gone for long stretches. She didn't like being alone and she sure didn't like me being around all the pretty girls that hung around my employer. We broke up soon after. She ended up marrying a doctor. I'm told they're very happy."

"That's awful. I'm so sorry that happened to you."

Leaning forward, he rested his elbows on his knees. "I was hurt at the time but looking back I can see she had a valid reason. It's hard to have a relationship when only one of you are there. I was focused on my work and finding Gigi and Aubrey. I didn't make her a priority. She wanted a more settled life with a man who could make her feel secure and special. She'd had a rough childhood like I did and she wanted the fairytale. I'm glad that she's happy."

Leann could understand the other woman's doubts but it was hard to imagine anyone leaving Zach for that reason only.

"What about you? Have you ever been engaged or close to it?"

"No, I haven't." Leann shook her head, a little sad at the thought. "I did have a long-term relationship that lasted four years but surprisingly we never discussed marriage. He was proud of the fact he was a live-in-the-moment kind of guy. At the time I was fine with that. I was young and not looking to get tied down so it wasn't a problem. Later as I became more involved with my career it was harder to nurture a relationship. I dated but the longest relationship was about six months. Wow, that makes me sound like a giant loser. It's just that as I grew older it was easier to see when it wasn't going to work out with a man. There was no reason to keep dragging things out when it was only going to end. Probably badly too."

Maybe this honesty stuff wasn't all it was cracked up to be.

"It think it's the same for me. I can tell by the first date if there's going to be any spark." Leaning over, he pressed a kiss to her lips, sending a bolt of lightning to her curled toes. "So I'll ask you the same question. What's wrong with you? What would you hope that I never find out about you?"

Wrinkling her nose, she took a sip of her wine for courage. "I snore. I'm impatient. When I want something I want it now. I like the house to be clean but I hate actually cleaning it. I'm addicted to chocolate and caffeine, and I can be moody. Oh, and I have a temper. According to my brothers, it's a nasty one."

"All of that doesn't sound too bad. I think we can all be moody at times and I love chocolate too. I don't like to clean either. As for a temper, I think I'm rather easygoing but I can get angry. Your brothers might be exaggerating."

Sadly, they didn't.

"No one has ever described me as easygoing."

Zach wrapped his arm around her and pulled her closer. Snuggling into his chest, she could smell his scent mixed with the aroma of cut grass. "There's nothing wrong with being intense as long as you know when to relax."

She could feel the steady beat of his heart under her palm lulling her into a serene state. "I'm relaxed now."

"Then just lie back and enjoy the peacefulness of the night. Can you hear the crickets? They're playing us a song."

"I didn't realize you were a romantic."

One more thing that made him wonderful.

"It's hard not to be when I sit out here and look up at the stars with a beautiful woman in my arms."

"Flattery will get you everywhere."

"I'm counting on that."

It felt like forever until his lips touched hers, but her reaction was instantaneous. Leann couldn't seem to get close enough, straining to press her body to his. Despite the coolness of the evening, the blood swept through her veins bringing with it a sizzling heat that burned her flesh. Her palms rested against his chest before winding around his neck, her fingers carding through his short, dark hair.

The beating of her own heart pounded in her ears, perfectly in sync with his. At some point he'd moved her onto his lap and his hands stroked her back, her neck, her hips, anywhere he could reach while his lips traveled from her mouth down to the spot where her pulse beat at the base of her neck. Melting into each other, Leann had to hold onto his shoulders while they kissed. The earth had sped up on its axis, seeming to steal the breath from her lungs.

When he finally pulled away, both their breathing was ragged and labored. Torn between throwing herself at him and being cautious, her mind argued back and forth regarding the virtues of both of those plans. She didn't want to rush into being intimate with Zach but already she felt more for him than she had any man in a long, long time. He seemed to understand her dilemma as they gazed into each other's eyes, their emotions stripped bare for the other to see. She wanted him, and it was clear he wanted her too.

It would be so easy to take his hand and lead him into the bedroom, make love with him. She wasn't hesitating because she didn't feel anything for him; she was hesitating because she felt so much. If she was intimate with him it was going to mean something, there was no doubt about that. She hadn't expected this when she'd come home to Tremont. She hadn't expected to maybe…fall in love. It was scary, far scarier than someone who wanted her dead.

Apparently he'd taken her silence for a negative answer, pulling farther away but his arms were still around her, strong and warm.

She wasn't saying no.

They were adults. The attraction between them was off the charts hot. But mostly she knew that Zach was a good and kind man. The fact that he was sexy as hell didn't hurt but surprisingly, it wasn't the main attraction. He made her feel beautiful, special, and cared for, something she hadn't experienced with a man in far too long.

Trailing her fingertips across his strong jaw, she ran them down his neck and across his broad shoulders. Her lips captured his again, their tongues playing a game of tag as his strong hands glided down her spine to her hips.

"Baby…" he breathed softly against her shoulder. "We don't have to–"

"We do," she laughed, her fingers caressing his lips. "I can't think of one good reason not to."

Chapter Twenty-One

ZACH AND LEANN fell onto the bed kissing and giggling as they pulled the covers back. His hands felt as if they were everywhere, tugging at her clothes until she was clad only in her panties and bra. A non-matching set, but Zach didn't seem to mind at all. His blue gaze was hot as it swept up and down her body from head to toe, making her skin tingle with arousal.

She reached for the buttons on his shirt. "Your turn."

His own impatient hands came up to assist hers. "You still have some clothes on, honey."

"We'll take care of it in a minute," she chided him, tossing his shirt on the floor and pressing her lips to his muscular chest. She kissed a wet trail all the way down his taut abdomen to the button of his jeans before popping it open and tugging down the tented zipper.

His own hands pushed his jeans down his powerful thighs and kicked them away, landing on top of his shirt. His black boxers followed immediately after, leaving him gloriously naked. His body was as beautiful as it was powerful, like a Michelangelo masterpiece in marble.

Zach grinned at her hungry perusal. "Like what you see?"

Her cheeks warm, Leann could only nod shyly as he pushed her flat onto the mattress, hovering over her. Zach reached behind her and unclipped her bra, flinging it carelessly over his shoulder without a second look. Bending his head, he drew a rosy peak into his mouth, licking and suckling at the hard nub before turning his attention to the other side. Arrows of arousal ran straight from her nipples to her clit and she twisted and squirmed underneath him as flames licked at her quivering flesh. They'd barely begun and she was already flying high in the clouds.

He slid down her body, gliding her panties down her legs and onto the ever growing pile of clothes on the floor. Zach pushed her legs apart and insinuated himself between them as his tongue nipped and licked at her inner thighs. Taking his time, he traced patterns on her sensitive skin before traveling to the place she needed him the most. Mewling with frustration, she twisted and bucked, her fingers curling into his silky dark hair.

Slowly and deliberately he explored her folds until she was begging for release. With every flick of his tongue, the coil of arousal in her belly tightened painfully and she'd long ago lost the ability to think or speak clearly. Her world had narrowed to the two of them and his talented mouth and fingers. Nothing else existed except the most exquisite sensations that only he could bring her. Her lids drifted shut, her chest rising and falling rapidly as her heart drummed against her ribs. Sweat bloomed on her skin and her legs trembled as she neared the peak. It wouldn't take much to send her over. A mere puff of his warm breath would do it.

His mouth closed over her button and he sucked gently, his

teeth gently scraping the sides and giving her a pleasure-pain moment. Leann froze for a moment, her torso bowed and her toes curled. Thrashing her head back and forth as the waves wracked her frame, she whispered Zach's name over and over until she finally drifted back to earth, wrung out but strangely not satisfied. She needed more. She needed Zach.

Leann's hand drifted down his torso, over his ribcage, skimming his ridged abdomen and down to encircle his thick cock. Long, thick, and hard, it felt like velvet under her fingertips and she stroked it up and down, drawing a ragged groan from Zach's lips. Smiling in satisfaction, she ran her fingers from the thick base to the reddish-purple head, watching in awe as he threw his head back and moaned. Heady with her own power, she did it again and again.

Scooting down on the mattress, Leann swiped her tongue on the head of Zach's cock, taking him deeply inside of her mouth as her hand encircled the thick base.

"Fuck, babe, that feels good." Reluctantly, he pulled away, her mouth sliding off with a pop. "I want to watch while you ride me."

It sounded hot but this wasn't Leann's favorite position. She never seemed to be able to get the rhythm right and it ended up feeling more awkward than sexy, but this was Zach and she was going to give it a try.

Stretching out on the bed, Zach reached into the nightstand next to the bed and retrieved a condom, rolling it on. Taking a deep breath, Leann threw a leg over his muscular thighs so she was straddling him, but he didn't immediately grab at her like other men had. He ran his hands up and down her thighs in a soothing motion and she felt herself relax under his tender ministration.

Zach was indeed watching her, his gaze almost a physical feeling on her skin. It wasn't unpleasant and she found that under his worshipful regard she felt sexy and beautiful. His admiration was clear to see in his expression and her urge to cover up and hide dissolved along with any remaining reservations. This was going to be different because it meant something. To both of them.

Her lids felt heavy and she gave in to their weight, letting them drift shut. Enshrouded in darkness her other senses came stunningly alive. The brush of the hair on Zach's legs against the sensitive flesh of her inner thigh. The subtle perfume of their combined arousal. The salty tang of his skin when she leaned forward to drop kisses on his neck and chest.

"It's your show, beautiful. We go at your pace."

Zach's voice was hoarse but controlled. He'd handed her the reins and she was infinitely grateful. Right now she needed to be the one in charge but soon she'd hand it over happily.

The tip of Zach's cock nudged her entrance but his reassuring words echoed in her brain, assuring her she could take her time. Letting gravity do the work, she stretched wide to accommodate him as he ran over a sensitive spot inside, and she paused to allow her muscles to get used to being so incredibly filled. It only took a moment for the discomfort to turn to pure pleasure.

Oh yes.

Zach's expression was tortured but to his credit he didn't reach out and slam her down on his cock. Not yet. He made do with planting a hand on each of her hips, the fingers flexing tightly as she continued to lower herself. Slowly, wanting to savor each moment. When she had every inch he had to give, she let her head fall back with a gasp. She hadn't expected to feel this much pleasure, but the tingles and sparks of arousal were already beginning to build toward a second peak.

Swiveling her hips experimentally, Leann was rewarded with a groan from Zach, heat and pleasure suffusing her entire body. She did it over and over until she was light-headed and Zach's hands clamped onto her hips.

"Ready to hand over the control, baby? Or are you enjoying calling the shots?"

She'd barely even answered when she gave out a yelp of surprise. In a split second she was flat on her back, Zach on top.

"Is this okay?"

Hell, yes.

"Do it," she answered breathlessly. Her body was already responding in its predictable way. Zach quickly took control of the lovemaking, his hands on either side of her body as he nuzzled her neck and shoulder. Each thrust was deeper, harder, faster, taking her breath away and sending her spiraling into orbit. Her entire being was on fire and she wrapped her legs around his lean waist as he powered into her, riding her hard until she thought she would fly apart from the maelstrom of pleasure each thrust evoked.

"More. Faster." Her voice was thin and needy but Zach heard the plea in her tone. Grunting with the effort, he built up speed, their bodies covered in sweat, increasing the unbearable tension inside of her until she exploded into a thousand pieces. Her nails dug into his back and she cried out his name as her soul flew around the room before splintering into a thousand shards of light.

Forcing her eyes to open, Leann watched as Zach thrust in one last time, his expression fierce, his head thrown back exposing the taut cords of his neck.

Softly, so quiet she almost didn't hear it, Zach said her name before collapsing on top of her. He gulped in a few deep breaths to feed his starved lungs before rolling onto his back and tucking her into his side. His hands – capable of such violence – were gentle as they stroked up and down her damp spine. He whispered sweet words that didn't make much sense at the moment, planting kisses on her forehead and temple in between.

Leann had been thoroughly made love to and now she was being cosseted and cuddled. She couldn't ask for more.

Except maybe round two.

In the morning, after they'd rested awhile. Her limbs were heavy and her eyes wanted desperately to close. She was giving it the good fight when she felt his chuckle rumble in his chest.

"Sleep, honey. I'll be right here when you wake up."

She wasn't going anywhere either. What she had here was better than anything before.

Chapter Twenty-Two

IT WAS THE smell that hit Zach first. The stench of death hung heavy over the old, decrepit barn. Deputies had been checking everywhere that Darrell Madison might be hiding out and abandoned buildings had been second only to the homes of friends and family. They'd hit the jackpot in the middle of the night.

Some kids had gone out drinking and partying and ended up making the grisly discovery. Zach had received the call from the police about one in the morning, which meant that he had to either drag Leann out of her warm, comfortable bed in the next room or find someone to watch over her. His next call had been to her brother Jason who had gladly taken the job.

The medical examiner crouched over the body of Darrell while Zach anxiously awaited his verdict, sipping on a hot coffee that he hoped desperately would wake him up.

"Gunshot wound to the chest is my preliminary cause of death."

Shot? If the killer had a gun, why didn't he use it on Drew? Assuming it was the same person, of course.

"Is there an exit wound or is the bullet still inside?"

"No exit wound. I'll send the bullet to the lab when I extract it. You can see if it matches this." He held up a gun with his gloved fingers. "This was sitting under the victim's arm. It could just be his, though, trying to defend himself."

Bagging the firearm, Zach examined it and saw that it had been fired recently. Had Madison got off a shot before he was killed? Perhaps there was an injured man wandering Tremont and he might end up in an area emergency room.

Naw, I'm not that lucky.

"Estimated time of death?"

The medical examiner stood to make way for the men who would bag the body and take it to the morgue. "That's going to be a tougher question. He's definitely been here a day or two. I'm guessing late Saturday or early Sunday maybe."

"Thanks. Call me when you have anything."

The body was zipped into a bag and loaded onto a gurney before being rolled out of the ramshackle structure. Now that Madison was on his way to autopsy, Zach walked the perimeter of the barn looking for anything unusual or out of place.

"There are tire tracks in the back."

Looking up, Zach wasn't surprised to see West standing there. Jesus, the man needed a hobby or something. Did Gigi even know her husband had escaped the house?

"Tim, can you get photos of the tracks and then make impressions?" Zach asked one of Tremont's junior detectives before approaching West. "Is there something I can do for you?"

West rolled his eyes at Zach's careful tone. "You can give me a rash of shit about being here. I have no good excuse and I know you can handle this, but my curiosity got the better of me when I got the news. I was going to call you into my office for an update in the morning and then found myself in the truck driving here to see it for myself."

At least West had had the grace to admit he didn't belong here. It also looked like he still had contacts in the police department to have been called in the middle of the night about Darrell Madison.

"You might want to see a doctor about those blackout periods, West. Could be dangerous."

"Might get my ass kicked, that's for sure." West grinned and pointed to the barn. "Found anything?"

Zach actually kind of felt sorry for West. It was clear his brother-in-law missed being a cop but it didn't look like he'd get to go back to it any time soon. The town was thrilled with the job he was doing as mayor and were already pressing him to run again.

"Just got started. Wouldn't mind a second set of eyes."

That smile grew wider. "Don't mind if I do."

They started inside where the body had been found. A large pool of blood was located in the corner indicating where the shooting had occurred.

"So Darrell stood here." Zach put himself in position. "Maybe he was facing the doorway? If he was expecting company he wouldn't have any reason to be worried about the killer being in between him and the only exit."

"That would make sense. He would probably need help to evade the law." West nodded and knelt down next to a stack of garbage. "It looks like Madison was hiding out in here. There's a change of clothes, a blanket, some empty water bottles, and food wrappers."

"I'll have Tim bag all of that. Where is the food from?"

West used a pencil to sift through the trash. "Lucy's. Looks like had a couple of burgers, some fries, and a shake. Strawberry. I prefer the chocolate."

"Lucy's have a camera we can pull footage from?"

West stood and shook his head. "Not unless she's added it recently. Damn, that would have been useful. We could have seen who bought a similar order in the last few days and that might tell us who was helping him. He couldn't go there himself with the whole town looking for him."

There had to be a helper. There was no way Darrell Madison was going to waltz up to the nearest fast food joint, order himself some junk food, and then parade down Main Street as if he didn't have a care in the world. Not when the entire Tremont police force was looking for him.

"So if Darrell is our guy, then he shot Drew Marshall and came here to hide out. That makes sense. Someone was helping him and they may or may not be involved in the original murder but they might be the person who shot Darrell. I guess it's progress."

"Then you think Darrell killed Marshall?"

Zach grimaced as he studied the crime scene. "I'm not ready to say that yet. It's a definite possibility but Darrell could have been hiding out here simply because he was a suspect, not because he did it."

Crossing his arms over his chest, West nodded in agreement. "He might have been shot because he knew who the real killer was. Looks like we have two competing theories. How do we decide?"

Zach pointed to the door. "We've got tire tracks coming in and out of here. We'll see what make and model vehicle they belong to. We also found a firearm under the body. We'll see what ballistics can pull from it. Hopefully one of those two items will push us in the right direction. If not, there's always old-fashioned police work."

"What did you have in mind?"

"Time to talk to Darrell's soon to be ex-wife. What time do you think she gets up in the morning?"

✦ ✦ ✦

STRETCHING AND YAWNING, Leann padded on slippered feet into the kitchen. The heavenly aroma of coffee wafted around the house and she needed her caffeine fix soon. She had a big day ahead of her, although she hadn't discussed it with Zach yet. She was going to look at a house with Dizzy. Her friend was willing to pretend that she was looking to buy, not Leann. If it got out that Leann was looking at homes…

It would be bad. Very bad. Right now she simply wanted the killer found and some semblance of normalcy to return to the town.

Stopping abruptly in the kitchen doorway, Leann saw Jason sitting at the table, not Zach.

"How long was I asleep?"

Smiling, Jason hopped up from the table and crossed over to the coffeemaker to pour her a cup. "I have no idea, but it's about seven-twenty in the morning so you can do the math. If you're wondering where Zach is, we got the call in the middle of the night. Darrell Madison is dead. Shot in the chest. Zach is working the scene and any follow-up. I'm protecting you for now."

Leann simply could not drag her brother to look at houses. He might believe that Dizzy was looking for a new home but that wouldn't stop him from pushing Leann to move back.

Focus. Dead body found. Think real estate later.

"He's dead? Do you know who shot him?"

Jason shook his head. "We don't but there was a gun found. Ballistics will tell us if Madison tried to use it to defend himself or if it was the murder weapon."

Leann took a fortifying sip of her coffee. "Where does that leave us? Darrell was the main suspect. Do you have any others?"

Jason cleared his throat and tugged at the collar of his shirt. "No, and that means I need to shake things up a little bit in the investigation. Zach's only been working the leads part-time because his main focus has been protecting you, but I really need him to work this case one hundred percent. I'm planning to have one of my other men take over your protection duty."

It was all Leann could do not to burst into laughter. They'd really hit Jason where it hurt when she'd said Zach was considering moving to Florida with her. His best laid plans were slowly going up in smoke.

She shook her head. "I don't think so."

His jaw dropped and he blinked in surprise. "What do you mean? You can't say no."

Stretching out her legs, she gave him a serene smile. "Sure I can. Being protected was my choice to begin with. You can't force it on me. I was okay with it being Zach but I don't want anyone else. If Zach needs to work leads I'll simply go with him. I won't be any trouble."

Her brother paced the kitchen, his shoulders stiff. "I'm going to ask Logan to take over for Zach. He's a great guy and I trust him completely."

Leann had met Logan Wright and she trusted him too. But that wasn't the point.

"Why don't you have Logan chase down the leads then? Zach and I are used to each other. I don't want to have to start over with someone new. This living together stuff isn't easy."

Jason's gaze went to the staircase that led to the bedrooms. "Isn't it a little quick for you and Zach to be living together? I mean…that's a big step."

Older brother assumed she and Zach were sharing a bedroom.

"Frankly, that's none of your business, Jason. I don't ask about your sex life with Brinley because I sure as heck don't want to know about it."

His cheeks turning red, Jason shifted on his feet. "I'm just saying that I don't think you should rush into anything. You know, Zach's been single a long time and I doubt he's the marriage and family type. If you want to settle down someday he's probably not a good bet."

Seriously? Jason was going to try that line? Her brother was standing in the middle of the most domestic bachelor pad ever spouting a line of bullshit no one would buy.

"Actually, that's not the case at all. Zach definitely wants to have a family someday, and I think he'd be a wonderful father after all he's been through in his childhood. If I remember correctly, Brinley took a chance on you. I wouldn't have said you were exactly marriage material either when she met you."

Her brother seemed to stagger back and had to place a hand on the counter to steady himself. "Jesus, you've talked about marriage? Are you that serious?"

It was fun to torture her brother but she didn't want to be completely cruel. "In a very generic way, not in an 'us' way. We were simply talking about how he'd created a very comfortable home here for himself. That's it. We're not nearly close to getting hitched, so relax."

"Thank God. That would be fast even for you, Sis. Take your time. Get to know one another."

"How long did you give Brinley?"

"You've got me there. This is more of a *do as I say, not as I do* conversation."

Slapping her empty coffee cup down, Leann grinned at her brother.

"That's how I've lived my entire life, Jason. I'm not about to change now."

Chapter Twenty-Three

MELANIE MADISON WAS an attractive woman with light brown hair and light blue eyes that were currently watery and red-rimmed. Zach and West had personally delivered the news regarding her soon to be ex-husband.

Her hands fluttered nervously as the three of them sat down in the living room. "Can I get you some coffee? Or something…?"

Zach shook his head. "No, thank you, ma'am. We're fine. Is there anyone we can call for you? A friend or a family member?"

Tearing up again, she nodded. "My sister Amy. She'll come here to be with me."

West carefully held out his hand as if trying not to spook the woman. "Why don't you give me your phone and I'll give her a call? That's Amy Darden, right? I remember her from high school."

Melanie tried to smile and gratefully handed over her cell. "That's right. You're about the same age."

"I'll just give her a call."

West retreated to the other side of the room, leaving Zach to ask the questions. Of the two jobs, Zach thought he had the better one and God bless West for taking the more difficult task on himself.

"I'm sorry for your loss, ma'am," Zach began. There was really no way to make these questions impersonal. He was going to pick at a fresh wound whether he liked it or not. "You and Darrell were separated, is that correct?"

Sniffling, Melanie nodded. "We split up a few months ago. Darrell was drinking and gambling too much. He said it was the stress of running the ranch but it had become progressively worse these last five years. Finally I couldn't take it anymore."

"You said he was spending a lot of time out of the house. Do you know who he was hanging out with? Who were his friends?"

Dabbing at her eyes with a tissue, she shook her head. "I don't know. Whenever I tried to talk to him about it he'd just get upset and stomp off. Eventually I stopped asking, although I do think he started dating someone recently. He had all the signs."

"All the signs?" Zach repeated. "What kind of signs?"

"Suddenly he started caring about how he looked. New haircut. New shirts. He'd be clean-shaven when he came over to visit with the kids, which wasn't like him at all. He even bought new boots. He smiled more too. The only thing I can think that would work that sort of magic was a new woman."

It didn't appear to bother Melanie that Darrell had possibly found a new female but clearly from her reaction to his death she'd still cared about him.

"Did you ask him about it? Did he ever mention a name, even in passing?"

"No, I didn't and he never brought it up either. I was just

happy to see him halfway sober. He'd been brooding since the day I'd ended it."

Zach scratched down a few notes. "I'm almost done here, ma'am. Darrell still worked the ranch, right? So he was here every day?"

"From sunup to sundown. He still had a key to the house so he could come in here and have some lunch. I was hoping he and I could be friends when all the legalities were over."

The cops were pulling apart Darrell's cramped apartment in town but if he wanted to hide something, he might do it here where he would think no one would look.

"Ma'am, do you mind if we search the house and property? I'm not sure what we're looking for but Darrell may have left some clues as to who murdered him."

Melanie nodded vigorously. "Whatever you need to do. I want to find out who did this, if only for my children's sake." Fat tears squeezed through her lashes. "They're at school right now. I guess I should pull them out so I can tell them."

"Maybe your sister can help you with that," Zach gently suggested. This woman had enough on her plate to deal with.

"That's a good idea," she rasped. "I'll ask Amy's husband to go get them. I still can't believe this is happening. Do you think Darrell killed all of those people?"

That was a good question but he had a better one. "Do you, ma'am? Was Darrell capable of taking a life?"

"No," she said firmly. "No, he wasn't. The Darrell I loved and married never would have done something like this. He couldn't have unless his own life was threatened or he was protecting me and the children."

"Thank you, Mrs. Madison." Zach stood and was joined by West, who handed the phone back to Melanie. "We'll be in touch if we have any more questions, but if you don't mind we'd like to start looking through Darrell's things. Is that okay?"

"It's fine." Her attention swung to West. "Did you get a hold of my sister?"

West nodded. "She and her husband are on their way here. It won't be long. How about I sit with you until they arrive?"

Zach's brother-in-law could be a real gentleman when he wanted to be, and the brand new widow seemed to take comfort from his presence. With West occupying Melanie, Zach headed straight for the garage to search through Darrell's things. He didn't expect to find anything of substance but he wasn't going to let this chance pass.

Maybe, just maybe, Darrell left them a clue.

IT HADN'T BEEN easy getting rid of Jason but she'd convinced him that he was needed on the murder case and not tagging along with her and Dizzy. Instead, he'd assigned two of his newer investigators to accompany her until Logan Wright arrived into town, which was supposed to be tonight. Leann liked Logan just fine but she was determined to stay with Zach. The two new men, however, were friendly and didn't try to push their way into her day to day business. While she and Dizzy looked at houses, one of them sat in the car and the other walked the perimeter looking for bad guys.

Those were his actual words to her. *Perimeter. Bad guys.*

Dizzy checked the list in her hand. "Is this the first one today?"

"We're seeing three but this one looked the most promising based on its location. What do you think?

The real estate agent pushed open the white-washed wooden gate and ushered them into the home's large front lawn. The house had been empty for quite awhile so the yard needed some tender loving care. Leann could picture a colorful flowerbed to her right and a swing on the front porch once the outside had been given a fresh coat of paint.

"It's nice," Dizzy conceded but Leann could tell the jury was still out on this one. "Lots of trees and the neighbors look like they keep up their property well."

"The home is ready for immediate occupancy and the seller is very motivated," the agent said to Dizzy brightly as she unlocked the front door. "I'll give you a tour."

"Actually," Leann began, shooting a glance to Dizzy who was studying a broken flower box on the windowsill. "Would you mind if we nosed around by ourselves first? We won't take long. Then you can come in and show us what you think are the highlights."

The older woman shrugged. "I guess that would be fine. I have a few calls to make anyway."

"Thank you," Leann replied, linking her arm with Dizzy's and dragging her inside. Dust tickled her nostrils and she wrinkled it to keep from sneezing. "Okay, do your thing."

Wandering the perimeter of the living room, Dizzy gave Leann a disgusted look as she ran her fingertips along the walls and furniture. "It's not an actual skill like juggling. I can't order it up like a pizza. It's a feeling that just overtakes me. I can't explain it, it just *is*."

Leann wasn't even sure she believed in *it* but if she was going to buy a house she wanted to cover all her bases.

They headed into the kitchen and Dizzy stood in the center of the room, her head back and her eyes closed. Finally she opened them and shrugged. "I got nothing."

"So it's not haunted or anything?"

Wrinkling her nose, Dizzy sneezed. "It's dusty, but as for residual spirits who have yet to pass into the light? Nah, I'm not feeling it. We could check upstairs. Did you hear anything about this place that would lead you to believe it was haunted?"

They ascended the stairs and ended up in the oversized master bedroom. "Old Man Graham passed away here at home. Heart attack in the garage. I don't want to buy a house that is haunted by him. He wasn't very nice to people and I doubt he's improved with death."

Old Man Graham had been known as a curmudgeon of a man when Leann was a child and Graham wasn't that old. Somehow though, he'd always been called Old Man Graham.

"His daughter is selling it? Doesn't she live in Denver?"

Leann nodded, noting the renovated master bath with a jetted tub and large separate shower. There were even double sinks. This property was the holy grail of real estate if Dizzy gave it the all clear.

"She does and she's priced it well, but for some reason no one has purchased the house. It's been on the market for three months. That makes me worry that there's something wrong with it that a property inspector won't find."

Rolling her eyes, Dizzy sputtered with laughter. "Like the

ghost of Christmas past? People call me eccentric and they think you're normal. Go figure."

"You are eccentric. Wonderfully sweet but eccentric."

"It's part of my charm. Now let's check the other rooms."

There were three other bedrooms and two more bathrooms. Leann was silent while her friend felt for vibrations or whatever the hell it was that she felt. A whisper in her ear from a spirit? A tap on the shoulder?

Dizzy leaned against the bathroom vanity. "I'm not picking up anything at all. If you're still worried, we can place some crystals in each room. Maybe burn some sage to clear the energy."

Leann had to laugh at the absurdity of the situation. She was having a potential property checked for ghosts because no one had purchased it. Her family would have a field day with this. "How about we get a Ouija board and just ask them to leave?"

Dizzy's expression turned serious in an instant. "Don't even go there. Those things are not to be messed with, Leann. You could summon something truly evil if you don't know what you're doing."

Now she really felt stupid. She'd been kidding but Dizzy was serious. Cue *Twilight Zone* theme.

"Um…it was a joke."

"You shouldn't make light of those things. Anyway, I don't believe you have a ghost here. I don't think that's the reason the house hasn't sold."

Spreading her arms wide, Leann looked around the room. "There has to be some reason then. This place is perfect."

Just like that, Dizzy had turned from concerned to amused.

"Perfect? Honey, I think I see why this place is still on the market. What frightens me – more than restless spirits by the way – is that you can't see it."

"I'm listening."

Dizzy wrinkled her nose and sniffed. "Do you smell that? It's a mildew smell. Which tells me there's been a water leak at some point." She pointed the ceiling in the hallway. "I'd bet my bottom dollar that the roof is the culprit. Look where the owner tried to paint over that spot on the ceiling. I bet it was a leak that turned the ceiling brown."

Leann did smell it now, and she could see the subtle change in the paint color. Damn, Dizzy was good.

"You can sniff out ghosts *and* mildew?"

Dizzy breezed past Leann and moved toward the stairs. "There are many facets to my personality which you should be aware of after all these years—a few of them are even practical. Let me add that in addition to the mildew the closets in the bedroom are small, the appliances in the kitchen need updating, and the deck in the backyard is rotting. The whole layout of the house is awkward and strange with too many walls and hallways. I'm not even sure what wall you'd put a television on in the living room. Why don't you tell me why you think this house is perfect because I have a feeling I've missed that part."

Okay, maybe the house wasn't *perfect.* It had been a contender on the list.

"The master bedroom and bathroom are pretty terrific."

"They are," Dizzy agreed. "Is that enough to overlook the other items you'd have to deal with? What else do you like about this place?"

Leann sighed in defeat. "It's the location. Close to you, close to town, on the road to the ranch. The location is what got me. I guess I just convinced myself that the inside of the house was great too."

"I have to admit you have a good point there. The location of this home is crazy excellent. If you're willing to put some elbow grease into the place it might be a good buy. How much renovation are you willing to do?"

Wincing at the thought of months of construction dust and dirt, Leann couldn't deny the obvious. "I bought my condo in Florida while it was being constructed so I have zero experience doing anything like that, so I'd say the answer is not much."

"Doesn't your family *own* a construction company?"

"They own just about everything in this town. Haven't you noticed?"

It was a fact that Leann had never been allowed to forget.

"Once or twice," laughed Dizzy. "But seriously, I'm sure your family can handle whatever would need to be done to this house rather easily. Heck, you could mow it down and start fresh. Make it exactly what you want."

"Then I'd be living in your spare room for months."

"And you're such a nightmare to live with," Dizzy teased, her smile widening. "You can stay with me as long as you need to but first I think you need to admit something to me and yourself."

Dizzy had a way of cutting through the bullshit in life and Leann had a feeling her friend was about to do it again.

"What would you like me to admit?"

"That you're still conflicted about moving home. That your

choice of homes is part of it. If you pick a house that needs a major renovation it gives you the opportunity to stay unsettled. You get to kind of feel like this move isn't permanent. You're hedging your bets. And come on…you brought me here to check for spirits? For real? Since when do you believe in ghosts? Did you see one on the beach or something?"

With a groan, Leann slumped against the bannister. "Who is the psychologist here? You're the flighty artist and I'm the doctor."

"Physician, heal thyself."

They clomped down the stairs and back into the living room. Leann could see the real estate agent through the window, pacing back and forth on the front porch and speaking animatedly into her phone.

"I'm scared," Leann finally said. "I'm scared I'm making a mistake. The closer I get to doing this, the more freaked out I get. I want to come home, I truly do, but I know that some things never change."

"What do you tell your patients when they say things like that?"

Dammit, Dizzy was turning into a one-woman Yoda.

"That the only thing they can change is themselves."

"Have you changed since you left?"

Interesting question. Leann felt that she had. She'd grown up and matured. Seen some of life's hard times and experienced many good ones. She hoped she was wiser to go along with the older.

"Being back here has thrown me for a loop. Suddenly I'm eighteen again. The reunion didn't help that, by the way."

Dizzy shuddered and grimaced. "I wouldn't be eighteen again for all the money in the world. I doubt you would go back either but you're welcome to if you think it's any better. Don't worry so much about what other people think. There will always be someone who refers to you as an *Anderson*. Forget about them. They don't know who you are inside. Do you think I don't know what people say about me? Eccentric is one of the nicer words they use."

"And it doesn't bother you?"

Dizzy's lips twisted. "I'm human, Leann, so of course it bothers me. I wish people took me more seriously at times. So often they blow off my opinions just because I'm different than they are. I get mad about it, too. Especially when it's someone that I think should know better…like your brothers or cousins. But then I remember what I learned in art school and it all makes sense."

"Are you going to share what they taught you?"

Laughing, Dizzy took a seat on the worn couch. "I was just thinking of the best way to explain it. Let me try this…human beings are programmed to classify things. It's in our DNA and it helps us make sense of the world. It's why so many people separate their candy by color before eating it. So anyway, people like to put other humans into neat little labeled boxes. It soothes their uncertainty. The friendly residents of Tremont have placed me in the category of 'sweet but eccentric'. You are 'an Anderson'. It's just their way of controlling their environment. Once you understand that, an artist can manipulate their work to capture the human eye. I'm sure you learned something similar when you studied psychology."

Leann had although it had been described a little differently, but the meaning was the same. This was human nature and not something that was going to change just because it ticked her off.

"So I'm stuck? I'll be classified however they want me to be?"

Dizzy giggled and pointed to the pacing woman on the front porch. "Look at the bright side. You get to classify them too. It's a two-way street. For example, how would you classify your gorgeous bodyguard Zach?"

Zach? He was…wonderful. He was a major plus about moving back. And she'd get to see him again tonight. Logan was going to have to find someone else to protect.

Chapter Twenty-Four

After a long morning of looking at houses, Leann was ready for a late lunch. Preferably with Zach. He was sitting in his office looking over some papers when she stuck her head in.

"Come on in." He stood and greeted her with a small kiss. Nothing too outrageous because this was his work, after all, but enough to let her know he was happy to see her. "Did you have a good morning? Where's Dizzy? I thought you two were looking at houses for her."

"Me and my two shadows dropped her off at her house. But I would really like you to get to know her. Maybe we can all have dinner together tonight?"

"That sounds like a great plan. Dizzy sounds like someone I need to meet."

Leann settled into a chair. "But I'm starved right now. How about lunch? Have you eaten yet?"

"I haven't," Zach grimaced. "I've been busy with Darrell's murder. West and I talked to Darrell's widow this morning and she said she thought he had a girlfriend. How about I fill you in over a couple of cheeseburgers?"

Leann wanted to hear all the details, especially about this mysterious girlfriend. If he'd had a woman in his life, why had he been so bitter the night of the dance?

"Perfect."

They'd barely made it to Zach's office door when Leann's phone buzzed insistently. Dizzy.

"Do you mind if I take this? It's Dizzy."

"Sure. Do you want some privacy? I can–"

Leann shook her head and accepted the call. "No need. She probably just forgot to tell me something this morning. Hey, Dizzy. What's up?"

"I think you and your attack dogs should come back to the house." Dizzy sounded slightly breathless and her voice shook. "Someone has been in here. I can tell. Specifically in the guest room where your things would have been if you were still staying here."

Clearly Zach had overheard Dizzy's words because his expression turned from pleasant and happy to dangerously dark. He held out his hand for the phone and Leann gratefully gave it to him. It was at times like this she was glad she had him and her brothers in her life. They had experience with these sorts of situations. Her own heart had sped up and she could see the tension in Zach's shoulders.

"Dizzy? Are you still there?" he asked, putting the phone on speaker and holding it so Leann could hear as well. "Don't touch anything. Just quickly walk out of the house and go across the street. I want there to be some distance between you and the house, okay? I'm going to call the police and then I'm going to come to where you are. Are you walking out?"

"I am," Dizzy confirmed. "I'm closing the front door now."

"Just move away from the structure and wait for me. I'll be there in a few minutes."

He ended the call and handed her the phone. "We need to tell your brother and call the police."

They were already rushing toward Jason's office. "Why did you tell her to cross the street and get away from the house?"

Pausing at the entrance to Jason's office, Zach took a moment to answer. "We don't know what this guy did or why he was there. I'm sure I'm overreacting but I want to be on the safe side. I asked her to move away from the house in case there's any sort of explosive device."

Leann almost fainted and the meager contents of her stomach rose into her throat. A bomb? If something happened to Dizzy because of her, Leann would never forgive herself.

Never.

✦ ✦ ✦

DESPITE DIZZY'S SOMEWHAT flighty reputation, Zach found her to be level-headed and calm when he and Leann arrived at the house. Jason and his partner Logan Wright, who had shown up just as they were leaving the office, followed along but they left the other two new investigators back at the office. The firm was still combing through the backgrounds of the victims, looking for any possible connections other than high school.

Two cop cars and a couple of firetrucks greeted them and Zach was happy to hear that the bomb squad was already inside sweeping the house. Leann had given her friend a huge hug and Logan had planted himself right next to the women as a human guard dog. No one was getting near them without going through him. That left Zach and Jason to talk strategy.

"Do you think they thought Leann was staying with Dizzy?" Jason asked as law enforcement directed traffic around their vehicles. This was definitely going to be on the evening news. Zach was shocked the local news station's van hadn't beat them to the scene.

"I do," Zach confirmed, stealing a glance at Leann. She looked a little shaken, though her concern wasn't for herself but her friend. She seemed stubbornly resistant to the idea that her own life might be in danger. As a psychologist she would have been having a field day with the denial if it had been in anyone else but her own head. "But why were they here? When Leann wasn't home why didn't they turn and leave?"

"Maybe they wanted to confirm she was staying there," Jason said through gritted teeth. The man looked livid, the veins on his neck visible. "So they knew if they came back that she would be there."

"You're thinking this was just a recon mission?"

It made sense. If the killer was unsure whether Leann was staying with Zach or Dizzy, they would want to make sure which it was. Zach had gone out of his way not to publicize that Leann was staying with him. For all the town knew, she was still at Dizzy's, but some people might have figured it out. They weren't hiding it, either. There was no point in a small town like Tremont where his neighbors knew his every move.

"I doubt he came here to kill Leann in broad daylight with the possibility of Dizzy being home too. No, I think he knew the house was empty. Dizzy uses her garage as an art studio so she parks in her driveway. All the killer would have had to see is the car gone."

The leader of the bomb squad strode over to where Jason and Zach were standing. "House is clear. You can go in."

Zach wanted to know exactly what the killer had touched. It might give him a clue as to what he was after.

"Dizzy? The house is clear and we can go back inside. Can you show me what you saw when you came home that let you know that someone had been in the house?"

"Sure, it was really obvious."

Leann hadn't said a word but she was watching Zach closely, perhaps trying to gauge his level of concern. She wouldn't freak out unless he was.

All five of them entered the home and Dizzy pointed to the large picture window in the living room that looked over the street. "That's the first thing I noticed. The curtains had been pulled closed but I had opened them this morning to let the sunlight in."

"Probably didn't want anyone outside to see them moving around in the house," Logan observed. "But they didn't put them back when they left. Maybe they were in a hurry?"

"It was the middle of the day," Leann reasoned. "With the position of the sun how much could passersby have seen?"

Jason pointed out of the window. "Shade trees in the front yard might make shadows visible."

"Who would think it wasn't me?" Dizzy asked, shaking her head. She'd been quite pale when Zach had shown up but now her color had returned. "I'm home in the summer during the day."

"Killer might have been in a hurry and didn't think it all the way through," Zach explained, moving deeper into the house. "What else was moved or changed?"

Dizzy led them down the hall. "My bedroom door was open. I always keep it closed because of the way the vents work but it was wide open. But it was the guest room that was the creepiest."

The door across the hall was also open and Zach entered the room, seeing what Dizzy meant. The drawers on the bureau looked like they had been hastily opened and then shut poorly. The lace runner on the top was askew and almost falling off the furniture. The closet door was open and there were only a few garments hung in it, mostly clothes that looked off-season. Dizzy probably used it for storage.

Leann lifted up a throw pillow from the floor and placed it back on the bed. "They were looking for signs of me living here. Clothes, personal items, anything that indicated that I was staying in this house."

Jason had turned a peculiar shade, a cross between nauseous green and furious red. It appeared he didn't know whether to be pissed as hell or sick to his stomach. Logan, on the other hand, had a smile playing on his lips. An instinctual lawman, he was known for listening to his gut. According to those who knew him well, he was never wrong.

"You want to tell us all why you think this is a happy event?" Zach invited. "I'd love to hear something positive right about now."

Logan grinned sheepishly and shrugged. "It's just that I think this is good. If he didn't know where Leann was staying that means he hasn't been watching her. That gives us the advantage.

He doesn't know her routines so he'll have to improvise if he wants to get close to her."

"I don't have any routines," Leann pointed out with a sigh. "I'm here on a long vacation."

"But you probably have fallen into habits even in the last few days," Logan replied. "You and Zach get up and have breakfast. Maybe you go into the office with him. You come home in the evening and sit down to dinner. On Sundays you attend the Anderson family dinner. Do you see what I'm saying? This guy doesn't know any of that. We can use this."

Zach was afraid of where Logan was going with this. "We are not using Leann as bait."

Jason started speaking as well, but Logan put up his hands in surrender. "I'm not suggesting that we do that. I'm saying that we can mix up her schedule on purpose every day. Keep this guy from getting too comfortable. I want him to feel like he never quite has a handle on where or what Leann will do at any given time."

Jason grunted. "That makes sense and we can totally do that. Or we can just send her back to Florida where she'll be safe."

That was a huge admission from a brother who was plotting to fix her up with a man just to get her to stay in Tremont.

"We don't know that will work," Leann said sadly. "They might just follow me. Besides, we don't want this killer to go underground, right? We want to catch them, and my presence can help with that."

"We are not using you as bait."

Jason's voice was loud and even Logan winced.

"I hate to say this out loud, bro, but her very existence is bait," Logan said with a grimace. "As long as she's here, they're going to try."

"Unless the killer is only in town for the reunion," Zach replied. "If he has to leave soon it's good for Leann but not so good for the case."

"Doesn't mean a thing." Logan shook his head. "He'll find a way. He's waited fifteen years, he can wait a little more. We have to find him now."

It was Leann's turn to look sick at the thought of having this hanging over her head for months or even years. No way was Zach going to allow that to happen.

"Do you think they'll come back?" Dizzy asked. "Should I put extra locks on the doors?"

"I doubt they'll come back," Zach answered. "They know Leann isn't staying here and we have no reason to believe that you're in danger. But I don't want to take any chances until we have this guy locked up. Is there somewhere you can stay where you'd be safe? You can stay with me and Leann at my house."

"I can stay with her," Logan piped up. "But first we need to make a trip to a hardware store. No offense, ma'am, but those are some of the flimsiest locks I've ever seen. We need to beef up your security for no other reason than your general safety. You're just begging for someone to rob you."

"This is Tremont," Dizzy giggled. "Half of the people don't even lock their doors."

"Then fifty percent of the residents have lost one hundred percent of their minds," Logan shot back. "If they knew what was out there…"

He didn't have to say any more. The town had seen too much death in the last few days.

Everyone seemed happy and satisfied with the arrangements except Jason. His brows were pinched and Zach could only describe his expression as glowering. Apparently his employer didn't like it when his plans were foiled.

"Now wait just a minute," Jason spit out. "This was not the plan at all. The plan was–"

"Yes, brother dear?" Leann crossed her arms over her chest, her toe tapping on the floor impatiently. "What was your plan?"

His throat working, Jason couldn't seem to get an answer out, which seemed to amuse Logan greatly. The grinning man slapped Jason on the back. "Looks like it's settled then. Since Leann is already comfortable at Zach's place, she stays with him. I'll move in here with Dizzy just to make sure she's safe as well. If Zach needs to work the case during the day, I can give him a break with Leann's protection. It's all good."

Shoulders slumped in defeat, Jason shook his head. "That wasn't the plan."

"Plans change. Roll with it," Logan chuckled, giving Zach a covert wink. "Now, where's the nearest hardware store?"

Leann linked her arm with Zach's. "A few doors down from the diner, which was where Zach and I were headed for a late lunch. Is anyone hungry?"

Dizzy's eyes lit up. "I could eat."

"Hell, yes," Logan said.

A small silence and then Jason sighed. "I missed lunch too. We can talk about the case and where we go from here."

So far they had dead bodies and little concrete evidence. The murderer was working cleanly but was overdue to make a mistake. And when he did? Zach would be right there to catch him. All he needed was one little break in the case.

Chapter Twenty-Five

ZACH WAS ENJOYING a slice of apple pie after his cheeseburger when he received an email from Jared. The other partner in the firm had been burning up his laptop trying to find out all the minute details for each victim.

"Jared just sent me the preliminary report on Darrell."

"And?" Leann prompted. "What does he say?"

"It does appear that Darrell was seeing a woman but he can't tell who it was. Yet. There were out of town hotel rooms, purchases of wine and flowers, even condoms."

"So this woman might know who killed Darrell?" Dizzy asked.

"She might," Zach conceded. "He may have mentioned something or someone to her."

"Pillow talk," Jason echoed. "Men will reveal all sorts of secrets when they aren't thinking straight."

"Which is most of the time," laughed Logan. "Does Jared say anything about Darrell's phone call history? That might give us a clue."

Scanning the report on his phone, Zach nodded. "Mostly just the people you would expect. His ex-wife, his ranch suppliers, his sister in San Francisco, but there is one number that he called quite a bit this last month. A throw-away cell phone. Now isn't that interesting?"

Darrell Madison moved up several notches on Zach's suspect list. He hadn't been convinced before but this one item pushed him toward that conclusion.

Logan's fingers tapped the surface of the table. "So let's see what we have here… Darrell has a girlfriend. A girlfriend, according to our Jared, that he never calls. Could she be behind the untraceable cell phone? And why would she have one?"

Dizzy frowned. "Maybe she's married."

"That's how I'd do it if I was cheating on my husband," Leann agreed. "I'd keep everything separate. Calls, credit card charges. I'd go to an out-of-town motel too, just like Darrell did. Remember, he was already separated from his wife so he didn't need to sneak around."

"Or this person just doesn't like cell phone contracts," Jason cut in. "It doesn't have to be nefarious. It could be completely innocent. I'm not saying it is, but it could be. I just don't want us to get ahead of ourselves."

Logan chuckled and took another bite of his pie. "Hell of a coincidence. What else do we know? Darrell was shot by someone he trusted. Someone he wasn't afraid of, presumably from the crime scene. And since he was shot, he could have been killed by a man or a woman."

"But Bitty had to have been killed by a man," Zach pointed out. "A woman couldn't have subdued her so easily. There was barely a struggle."

"And Carole," Jason said, tapping his fork against his plate.

"She was killed by a tire iron to the head. That says male to me."

"Wasn't Carole drugged?" Leann queried, her brows pinched together. "If she could barely stand she would have been an easy target, man or woman."

Zach nodded in agreement. "And once again, she had to have trusted her attacker because why else would she go behind the bar into that dark parking lot unless she did?"

Leaning forward, Dizzy placed her iced tea glass down on the table. "I think it was a woman. I wouldn't go out someplace dark with a man I only kind of knew. An acquaintance. He'd have to be either my father, husband, boyfriend, or someone I'd known for years. But a woman? I doubt I'd think twice about it, but of course now that I've said this I certainly will. My new motto is *trust no one.*"

Dizzy made a compelling argument. A woman who was woozy and drugged would trust another female far more easily than she would a man.

"What about Drew's murder?" Leann asked. "Man or woman?"

Stroking his chin, Zach pondered the question. "There was little sign of struggle and only a few defensive wounds. I believe Marshall was taken by surprise. He wasn't subdued in any way and the killer was close to him to be able to do this. Really close. Marshall trusted them. So I guess you could say it could have been either one."

"It could have been someone from the party," Dizzy said. "Who had opportunity?"

Zach had been all through this part. "Lots of people, but opportunity is only one part of the equation. After killing Marshall, the murderer would have been covered in arterial spray. No way he or she could stroll back into the party clean and tidy. He'd either have to leave the building immediately or have a supply of clothes stashed somewhere to change into, and we looked for bloody clothes in every dumpster for a ten block radius. Of course, he or she could have taken their clothes with them."

Logan signaled the waitress for a coffee refill. "Then let's go with the theory that he or she had to leave immediately. Is there a back door they could have snuck out so they didn't see anybody?"

"Yes," Zach replied, running images of the hotel through his mind. "He could have exited by a back door and driven away. If we ever find Darrell Madison's truck we can test it for blood."

Jason's gaze darted around the table. "So are we saying we think there could be two murderers working together? A man and a woman?"

"Wait," Leann said. "You think that Darrell and an unknown woman did these murders? And then she killed Darrell? Why would she do this? What's her motivation? And why kill her partner in crime?"

"It's possible. Maybe she's another female from the reunion," Zach replied. "And this was some sort of revenge plot for their lives not working out the way they planned. As for why she killed Madison? Perhaps he was having second thoughts or maybe that was the plan all along. Confuse the cops with murders that could only be done by a man and then kill the patsy. Darrell Madison takes the blame."

Dizzy blew out a slow breath. "Except my home was broken into after Darrell's body was found. That means she – or he –

isn't done, right? The unknown gender killer has another name on the list."

"This is whole bunch of conjecture," Leann observed. "And not a lot of evidence. As Jason said the cell phone could be a complete coincidence, and his girlfriend knew nothing about what he was doing. Or not doing. We don't even know for sure that he was involved in the murders. We only think he was."

Too many questions and few answers.

"We know what to do now," Logan said. "We go back to the beginning and review everything. Somewhere the killer, or killers plural, left a clue. But one thing is for sure, if Darrell was involved, he wasn't alone. We know that because of Dizzy's break-in. Unless you believe in coincidences, which I don't. Not for a second. I'll add this as well. Whoever did break into Dizzy's place…they're an amateur. A pro wouldn't have made so many rookie mistakes. I don't think we need to go looking for previous murders that don't seem connected to these. This person has had some luck on their side but that always runs out."

The group finished their desserts quietly, all of them ruminating on the theories they'd discussed. Zach was frustrated but Logan was correct. This was exactly the right time to go back and review everything, especially now that they had some context after Dizzy's break-in.

They all left the diner and headed for the vehicles but Zach held Logan back for a moment.

"Thanks for looking after Dizzy. Jason had other ideas."

Logan looked like he was trying not to laugh. "Giving Jason shit is what I live for. He told me his plan and why, by the way. I mentioned it to my wife Ava and she hit the ceiling. Lectured me that Jason shouldn't be trying to manipulate his sister like that. She was so upset I had to remind her that I wasn't the one doing it. Anyway, I agree with her and think Jason is being a pain in the ass. Leann seems happy staying with you and just the little that I've talked to Dizzy, I can tell she's going to be fun to protect."

Zach shook his head. "This case is…"

"Yep, I can see that. We'll go over all of the evidence again. We'll find something. But there is something I think we should do. Might be too late to do it today but maybe tomorrow morning."

"I think I know what you're going to say. We need to go to that motel and see if we can get an identification on the female."

Logan grinned. "Bingo. Do we have photos from the reunion? We could take the desk clerk pictures of the women."

"We do," Zach confirmed. "In the meantime let's hope ballistics tells us something. I'm tired of coming up empty everywhere we turn."

Hopefully, Logan was right. The killer's luck was bound to run out eventually.

Chapter Twenty-Six

LEANN TOSSED AND turned, exhausted but not able to fall asleep. While her body might be tired her mind was going a mile a minute. She couldn't stop the images that ran through her mind, keeping her awake. All her classmates, people she'd called her friends. Was one of them a killer? Would they come after her next?

She wasn't afraid. Zach and her brothers wouldn't allow anyone to get close to her, plus growing up with boys everywhere she'd learned early to defend herself and take no shit. She'd like to think she could handle herself if someone came after her but she was probably fooling herself. If someone surprised her she would be screwed.

Padding downstairs, she poured some milk into a mug and placed it into the microwave to heat. Zach had some packets of hot chocolate mix and although it wasn't her mother's recipe, it was close enough. Elaine Anderson had always sworn by warm milk when Leann couldn't sleep. The chocolate was simply a delicious bonus.

"Can't sleep?"

Zach's deep voice had Leann jumping with surprise and

clutching her chest where her heart raced way too quickly. "Holy hell, you scared me. Do you always sneak around like that?"

"How can I sneak around my own house?"

Pressing a hand to her forehead, she sighed. "I don't know but you frightened the hell out of me. What are you doing up?"

"That was my original question." The microwave happily chirped that it was done. "So I'll ask again. Can't sleep?"

Retrieving the mug, she poured the powder into the milk. "My brain won't let me rest so I came downstairs for some warm milk."

"And chocolate. Good plan."

She stirred her cocoa and settled down at the table, wrapping her hands around the heated mug. "So we're clear why I'm awake. What's your story?"

"I woke up and you weren't there, so I came looking for you. I'm supposed to be protecting you, remember?"

"Is that the only reason you looked for me?"

Chuckling, he sat down next to her. "There might be a few other reasons."

"Such as?"

His fingers played with a long strand of her hair. "How about I've become used to you sleeping beside me in an obscenely short period of time? That I like the sound of you breathing and the smell of your shampoo? I even like the way you steal all of the covers, leaving me with nothing."

Her heart tightened, almost taking her breath away. How could a big guy like Zach get away with saying such romantic words?

It was true, though. They'd become incredibly close in a

short period of time. This week wasn't the first time she'd met Zach, far from it. But it was the first time she'd allowed herself to get to know him and so far she liked everything she'd seen. When they were together, they had fun. When they were apart, she couldn't wait to be with him again. She liked him, she respected him, and she craved him. His touch was addictive but so was his wicked sense of humor. He was settled and down to earth and he made coming back to Tremont very seductive.

Was this love?

She wasn't a person who believed in love at first sight, which this definitely was not. But in the last week she'd spent more time with Zach than if she'd been dating anyone else three or four hours at a time. This was almost speed dating on steroids. Lock the two of them up together twenty-four-seven and see if they can survive.

Frankly, Leann wasn't ready to put a name to the blossoming emotion inside of her. It felt too new, too fragile.

"I don't steal the covers," she retorted, sipping her cocoa. "You kick them off. As for the sound of my breathing, is that a nice way to say I snore? Because I totally don't."

"Whatever you say, honey. I'm just here to agree with you."

Rolling her eyes, she stood and rinsed out her cup before placing it in the sink. "I know better than that."

Zach stood as well, crossing the small kitchen to pull her into his arms, strong and solid. He made her feel so safe and cared for when they were like this. If only she could always feel this way, but that wasn't how life worked.

"Are you sleepy yet?"

She shook her head. "No, but maybe if I lay down the warm

milk will do its magic."

"We can watch a movie," he suggested. "There's nothing worse than lying in bed but not being able to sleep."

"Nothing with car chases or excitement."

Laughing, Zach led her up the stairs. "One boring movie coming right up."

✦ ✦ ✦

THE MOVIE WAS as boring as Leann had hoped it would be but she still couldn't sleep. Too many thoughts were racing around in her head like the Roadrunner and Wile E. Coyote. It was just going to be one of those nights. She didn't have insomnia often but when she did it came on with a vengeance.

Cuddling closer into the warmth of Zach's body, she tucked her head into the crook under his chin. His rough whiskers tickled her forehead and she reached up and ran her fingertips over his stubbly jaw, only to have him turn his head and nip at them playfully. Giggling, she pulled them away and sat up, leaning forward to give him a long, slow kiss. A delightfully naughty idea came to her.

If she couldn't sleep, maybe she could find something to occupy her time…

One of his hands had tangled in her hair while the other slid up under the oversized t-shirt she was wearing to caress the bare flesh underneath, sending tingles straight to her lower belly. Zach apparently had the same carnal thoughts. Great minds think alike.

"Zach," she sighed against his mouth, running her tongue over his lower lip. "Yes."

"We're going to miss the movie," Zach growled, trailing kisses down her neck and making her tremble with the onslaught of pleasure his touch evoked. "We don't know how this ends."

Hooking her thumbs in the waistband of his boxers, Leann tugged them down over his perfect backside. "We can Google it tomorrow. Besides, I know you haven't been watching."

"True. Let's get you naked."

Her nightshirt and panties joined his boxers on the floor even as his lips unerringly found the pulse point where her shoulder and neck met. The temperature in the bedroom seemed to zoom higher as liquid fire ran through her veins.

Time seemed to slow down as Zach's lips kissed every inch of skin from the top of her head to her ticklish toes. They had nowhere to be and all night to get there. With infinite patience, he learned every sensitive spot on her body and so did she. She'd had no idea that her instep or the curve of her hip were erogenous zones. That she'd shudder when his fingertips brushed the underside of her breasts or that his warm breath on her ear made her pulse pound. With every touch and caress the fire he'd started inside of her burned higher and hotter like a prairie fire out of control, consuming everything in its path.

His too talented tongue traced a line from her belly button to the valley between her breasts, sending shockwaves straight to her clit. Moving restlessly under him, her greedy fingers encircled his cock letting him know that she needed him now.

"Are you ready for me, baby?"

She'd been ready from the first moment he'd touched her. Whimpering at the loss of contact as he rolled on a condom, she welcomed him back to her with open arms. Her hands ran down his spine as he pressed inside of her, sweet and slow, just like their foreplay. When he was in to the hilt, he paused and gazed down at her, his pupils blown wide. There was such tenderness in his expression that she almost had to look away. It was intense and meaningful and her throat clogged with emotion so strong tears pricked the back of her eyes.

Leann didn't know if it was a mistake but she'd fallen in love with this man. She might have found her soulmate or she might get her heart broken into a million pieces, but she had a feeling it was far too late to back out now. He was everything she'd been looking for and a whole lot she hadn't even known she wanted.

Their foreheads pressed together and their gazes locked, he began to move out and then back in, leisurely at first and then faster to match their racing hearts and ragged breathing. With every stroke, he rubbed sensitive spots that sent her spiraling higher into the stratosphere. Leann was standing on the edge of a cliff, her toes hanging off, safe in the knowledge that when she fell she wouldn't be alone. Zach would be there to hold onto.

When her climax hit, the room spun while the lights behind her lids turned bright white. Her toes curled and her body was awash in pleasure as she clutched onto his strong shoulders like an anchor in a storm. His own release came immediately after and she watched fascinated as his jaw tightened and his eyes closed with pure bliss. He was the perfect combination of fierce warrior and contented lover, although the latter was winning the battle. With a groan of satisfaction, he rolled onto his back, taking her with him. Leann laid her head on his chest, happy to hear the steady thump of his heart under her ear. They didn't move for a long time, simply enjoying the quiet and the closeness.

“Do you want to watch the rest of the movie?” he asked eventually, his arm still wrapped around her, keeping her close to his side. His warmth was making her decidedly drowsy and after the mind-blowing orgasm she might just fall asleep after all.

A huge yawn sealed the deal. “Can we watch it tomorrow?”

“Of course.” He dropped a kiss on the top of her head. “Sleep tight, baby.”

She would but tomorrow she’d have to look herself in the mirror and admit she’d fallen in love. It was scary, handing over her heart to someone else. Trust wasn’t something that came easy, but then love hadn’t either until she’d met Zach. Everything was changing and she wasn’t sure she was ready for it. She only knew she needed him in her life.

Chapter Twenty-Seven

ZACH COULDN'T WIPE the happy smile off of his face. Whistling a lilting tune, he bounded down the stairs two at a time, anxious to see Leann again even though it had only been about twenty minutes since the last time.

After last night's lovemaking, he was sure Leann was the woman for him and he couldn't get enough of their time together. He'd been so close to saying "I love you" when they were cuddling but it had felt like the wrong time to reveal his growing feelings. He didn't want her to think he was saying it because of the sex. That wasn't it at all. When this case was finished, he'd fix her a romantic meal and tell her with some champagne and candlelight. She deserved more than a confession after sweating up the sheets.

When he hit the bottom of the stairs, he could hear her on the phone.

"The house was nice but I'm worried about all the needed renovations. I'm just not sure I have the patience for that."

Leann and Dizzy had looked at houses but it sounded like she hadn't found one she was sold on. He'd been through the renovation grind so perhaps he could give her some advice.

“I’m not pulling the trigger on any purchase right now,” Leann continued. It was probably Dizzy on the other end. “I go back to Florida at the end of the week and there is still a great deal to decide. I don’t want to rush into anything that I’ll regret later.”

Was he one of those things? A knife-like pain had taken up residence in his chest as he listened into a conversation he wasn’t sure he was supposed to be privy to.

“I’m just not ready to buy a house. Things are so unsettled.”

It was time to make his presence known. Clearing his throat, he brushed past her into the kitchen to pour himself some coffee.

“Listen, Dizzy. Can I call you back later? Okay. I will. See you then.”

Leann hung up the phone as he added cream and sugar. Smiling, she stood on tiptoe to press a kiss on his cheek and then slid her arms around his waist. She smelled amazing as usual, all fresh and clean from her shower. He buried his nose in her silky tresses and inhaled the soft scent of coconut, an aroma he would forever link to her from now on.

“So what’s the plan for today?” she asked, pulling back to pop a few pieces of bread into the toaster. “Dizzy said that Logan wants to visit that motel and see if they saw Darrell’s girlfriend.”

That was indeed what Zach had planned for the morning, but he was just stupid enough to bring up her phone conversation instead of moving on to the new subject. He wasn’t into head games or beating around the bush. Straightforward and honest was how he tried to live his life and in this he didn’t know how to be any different. He had to know the truth.

“I overheard you say that you’re not going to buy a house.”

Turning away, he couldn't see her expression as she stuck her head into the refrigerator to retrieve the butter. "Um…yeah. I haven't seen anything that makes me want to put in an offer."

"So you do want to buy a house? You just haven't found the right one."

That was completely different and he welcomed misunderstanding what she'd said.

"Eventually," she said, bustling past him and lifting the hot toast and dropping it onto a plate.

"Eventually," he repeated. "So you think you'll just stay with Dizzy for awhile then?"

"Dizzy offered to let me stay with her."

Leann hadn't answered his question.

"So is that the plan?" he persisted. "What about your place down in Florida? Are you going to put it on the market or maybe rent it out?"

Zach was pushing her, he knew that. Leann was going to push back. It was in her nature and a tactic she'd learned young with all those brothers and cousins, but he couldn't seem to stop himself. He needed to know that she was going to be around, that this relationship wasn't simply some vacation romance.

That it meant something. Because to him it meant a great deal.

"I don't know yet. That's a big decision." She paused, spreading butter on her toast. "Why all the questions?"

Zach could pretend it was just idle curiosity but that would be a lie and no relationship could survive that way.

"It kind of looks like you're still waffling back and forth about moving here, but you told me that you'd made the decision. Have you?"

Her cheeks turned pink and her gaze dropped to her plate. Not a good sign. "Sure I have. I'm moving home. I told you that."

"But you haven't told your family yet," he reminded her, taking in the way she fidgeted in her chair. If she was a suspect in the interrogation room he'd be wary of anything she was saying.

"I will."

"When? This Sunday at dinner?"

Huffing, she shrugged her shoulders. "Soon."

Her phone was sitting right on the table between them. Without even being aware he'd done it he now had her cell in his hand, holding it out to her.

"Call them. They'll be thrilled to hear it. What are you waiting for?"

Zach couldn't seem to stop himself, although he knew this wasn't going to end well. He was feeling insecure as if the ground was slowly giving way underneath his feet. He'd gone out on a limb with Leann but it looked like he was out there all alone.

She dropped her toast onto the plate, the color in her cheeks higher. "Why are you pushing this, Zach?"

"Why are you delaying?" he shot back, that pain in his heart more acute than before. "I think it's because you're still…after all this time…not sure about coming back. You're not sure about me."

Rolling her eyes, she groaned and jumped up from the table. "Don't make this about you. This isn't about you at all."

"Then tell me what it is about. Tell me what's holding you

back. Maybe I can help."

Leann didn't seem to know what to do with her hands, and eventually she shoved them in the pockets of her jeans. Maybe what she really wanted to do was smack his face for giving her a hard time.

"It's none of your business."

That knife in his chest twisted slowly, the agony excruciating. Whatever had been growing between them had just been cut off at the knees with that one statement. He was incredibly glad he hadn't revealed his feelings last night. Clearly she didn't share them. Already he could feel the distance growing between them, all because he'd dared to ask about her moving home. The nerve of him, wanting to know when his girlfriend was going to live in the same town.

He finished off his coffee and stood from the table. "I'll be ready to leave in five minutes. I'll drop you at the office. You and Dizzy can spend the day with Jason while Logan and I chase down a few leads."

Tuning on his heel, he headed upstairs, not allowing himself to look back. Leann was too afraid to move home so falling in love was probably out of the question. He couldn't take a chance on her if she wasn't willing to take a chance on him.

THE CONVERSATION HAD spun out of control so quickly and Leann hadn't been able to stop it. With a pit of despair in her belly, she watched Zach's retreating figure disappear upstairs, leaving her alone in the kitchen. Alone. If she wasn't careful that was exactly how she was going to end up. A cranky old woman with cats telling kids to get off of her lawn. Except she wouldn't have a lawn because she couldn't seem to get her shit together and make the commitment to move home and buy a house.

"What is my problem?" she muttered under her breath.

Leann wanted to move home. She'd made the decision and it was a done deal. There were a myriad of details to work out – her job, her condo and other smaller decisions – but she'd get through them one by one. She was excited about returning home to be closer to her family, Dizzy, and Zach.

But when he'd handed her that phone she'd froze, unable to make the call that would change everything. Her family would be thrilled and then they'd start "helping" her, but their help always came with a heaping dose of pressure. She wanted to do this on her own terms but her hesitation had sent the wrong message to Zach. He thought she was backing out and that she didn't care about him. Nothing could be further from the truth.

She'd screwed up royally by not voicing her fears to Zach. She wasn't, however, all that proud of the fact that she was hesitant and scared. She was a grown woman – at least that's what she kept telling her brothers – and at the moment it counted the most that she hadn't stood up, been honest, and admitted her weakness. If she was going to go around and whine that she was a grownup then maybe she ought to act like it. So far she'd done a piss poor job of it, acting like a child.

This was all about those boundaries she'd been trying to build. She should call her parents, tell them she was moving back, and then deal with whatever came after.

Like an adult.

It was beginning to dawn on Leann that the reason her family treated her like she was still a teenager was because she was acting like it. She'd been avoiding this very moment for years, taking the easy road. She'd done it again only a few moments ago when Zach asked her a perfectly reasonable question.

When are you going to tell them?

Now. She was going to tell them now. She'd start with Jason at the office and then call her parents. Words wouldn't fix this with Zach. He needed to see action and she'd give it to him.

She was moving home and it was far past time.

Chapter Twenty-Eight

ZACH PULLED HIS vehicle into a parking space near the front of the rundown motel located about thirty miles outside of Tremont in a little town called Elmville. He could see why Darrell chose this place. It wasn't too far to drive but it was enough out of the way that the residents of Tremont wouldn't know what was going on. Zach gathered up the folder of reunion photos to show the desk clerk.

"Do you want to talk about it?" Logan asked before Zach could open the car door. The former lawman had a shrewd expression that saw far more than Zach wanted him to.

"Talk about what?"

Shit, he sounded like Leann this morning. Now he knew how he had made her feel.

Put on the spot.

"You haven't said a goddamn word for thirty miles," Logan shot back. "But you gripped the steering wheel until your knuckles turned white. Maybe you should talk about it."

"I don't want to talk about my *feelings*."

Zach practically spat out that last word.

"Frankly, we're both men here and it's the last fucking thing

I want to do either, but as my wife Ava tells me every now and then keeping it all pent-up will make your pecker limp. I know you don't want that to happen, so for fuck's sake spit it out. Is it Leann?"

Zach had met Ava many times and the image of the little firebrand shaking her finger under Logan's nose and telling him his dick wouldn't get hard if he didn't speak up struck him as hilarious.

"I don't even want to know how that subject came up," Zach laughed, his shoulders shaking. "But yes, it is about Leann. She hasn't told her family yet that she's moving back."

"So?"

Dropping the file folder on top of the dash, Zach spread his arms out in frustration. "Why won't she tell them? What's holding her back? She says she's coming home but she won't actually say it."

"And you think she's lying?"

"Yes. No. Hell, maybe. I don't know. It just seems weird, that's all. And she doesn't have any plans made. She doesn't know if she's going to sell her house or rent it out. She hasn't made any progress in her plans."

When Zach said it aloud, his complaints sounded stupid and petty. The logistics of a move like that weren't something Leann was going to nail down in a week while attending her reunion and being stalked by a killer. He was now more than a little ashamed of how he'd acted this morning. She hadn't deserved his temper tantrum. But he'd felt…vulnerable. For the first time in a very long time he had serious feelings about a woman and he wanted her to feel the same.

"You could offer to help her with that," Logan suggested. "I would imagine the cost-benefit analysis on selling versus renting alone would be complicated. But that's not what this is all about, is it?"

"What if she doesn't move back?"

Logan pursed his lips in thought. "You travel constantly so you could visit her. Ava and I keep in touch on Skype when we can't be together. Modern technology makes it easier. I can read a bedtime story to the kids whether I'm physically with them or not but I'll say it again. That's not what this is about. Is it?"

"What if she doesn't feel the same?"

"Then you move on. Throw yourself into your work, get a puppy, take up a hobby. It'll hurt like a bitch but you'll survive."

Zach would survive but the process of getting over a woman like Leann wasn't going to be easy. Add in the fact that he'd have to see her every time she visited.

"Can we stop talking about our feelings now?"

Logan chuckled and swung out of the passenger seat. "Technically we were only talking about your feelings but let's definitely stop. If we continue we might end up hugging or some shit like that. In fact, after we finish here at the motel let's go get a beer and watch sports."

"It's nine in the morning."

"Then let's make it a whisky."

✦ ✦ ✦

IN JASON'S OFFICE, Leann sat across from her brother and spoke those three words.

"I'm moving home."

His eyes widened and his jaw went slack. After a few moments though, a grin spread across his face and he jumped up, rounding the desk to pull her into his arms for a big hug.

"Damn, Sis, that's great news! What changed your mind? Jesus, was it Zach? Are you two getting married?"

After what happened this morning the answer to Jason's last question was a resounding *no*.

Patting her brother's back, she tried to answer without revealing too much. "I am not getting married. I have been thinking about moving back for quite awhile now. I was planning on announcing it during this trip so the answer to your next question is I haven't told Mom and Dad yet. You're the first one. Well, except for Dizzy. And Zach."

Although he didn't believe her anymore.

"Dizzy and Zach knew?" Jason's brows pinched together. "Wait…I thought you said that Zach was going to move to Florida with you. Now you're moving here?"

"Zach was never moving to Florida."

No point in beating around the bush.

"But you said…? I'm not following you."

Leaning against Jason's desk, Leann crossed her arms over her chest and gave her older brother the meanest look she could muster. "Before I answer that, is there anything you want to tell me? Maybe about how you and West colluded to bring me and Zach together so I would move back to Tremont?"

Jason's face turned red and he suddenly found the carpet fascinating. "Well…shit. How long have you known?"

"Good on you that you didn't deny it. Zach and I have known for quite awhile, which is why I decided to mess with you and West a little bit. You deserved it. It's behavior like this that kept me in Florida all these years. What in the hell were you thinking?"

Jerking his head up, Jason scraped his fingers through his hair. "Christ, Zach knows? Is he mad? Shit, I don't need to lose my best employee over this."

Leann wagged a finger in Jason's face. "You should be more worried about losing a friend. You should have thought about that before you tried to manipulate the two of us. Zach hasn't said he's angry but honestly, I wouldn't blame him. If nothing else, he's our brother-in-law and it was a crappy thing to do. To both of us."

"I'll apologize to him. I will."

Raising her brows, she waited for him to go on but when he didn't she let out a heavy sigh.

"What about my apology?"

"I'm not sure you deserve one after the mean trick you played on me. I truly thought we'd failed and that you and Zach were going to Florida."

"I only did that because you were trying to control me. You have to stop doing that. I thought you were on my side, Jason."

His expression softened. "I am on your side, and I do want you home. Are those two ideas mutually exclusive? We miss you around here, little sis. It's not the same with you gone. We feel…incomplete. I want my kids to grow up with their Auntie Leann around."

A lump lodged in her throat as she thought about missing out on the new generation of Andersons growing up. "I want that, too. It's one of the big reasons I made the decision to move back."

"Was Zach part of that decision?"

Leann shook her head. "I'd pretty much already made the decision before I even came to the reunion."

It wasn't the entire truth but it was close enough. Jason didn't need to hear about the hours of soul-searching she'd spent going back and forth. Looking back, she was embarrassed it had been so difficult when the answer was so clear. She'd made it much harder and more painful than it needed to be.

Story of her life.

"So my plan didn't work? You and Zach…?"

Tears pricked at the back of her eyes and a sob broke from her lips. Her emotions were still too raw from this morning.

"I screwed up."

Holding out his arms, Jason beckoned to Leann. "Aww, honey. Come tell me all about it. Do I need to kick Zach's ass?"

She flew into them, unstoppable tears running down her cheeks. "No, you need to kick mine. I messed everything up and I don't know how to fix it."

"We'll fix it together," he said in his most soothing tone. "We'll figure it out."

"I think I might love him," she hiccupped, blindly searching for a tissue on his desk. "But he hates me now."

"I doubt that, princess. Zach isn't the kind that hates easily. Now why don't you start at the beginning and tell me what happened?"

✦ ✦ ✦

THE MANAGER OF the motel shook his head. "None of these

women look familiar. I really didn't see her. Just the back of her head. I only know that she's blonde. That's it. I'm sorry I can't help you more."

Logan slid a business card across the counter. "Thanks for talking to us today, and if you think of anything else, please call us."

"Will do," the man nodded. "Have a nice day."

Zach exited the motel office along with Logan as his phone buzzed in his pocket. It was Jason, hopefully, with the ballistics report from Darrell's shooting.

He didn't bother with greetings. "Please tell me you have some good news."

"Hello to you, too. Have you talked to the motel manager yet?"

Zach leaned against the side of the vehicle and held out the phone so Logan could listen in to the conversation. "We just finished and the only detail the guy knew was that she was a blonde. He never saw the front of her, only the back. We're hoping you have better news."

"Maybe. The firearm found under Madison's body was registered to him and it had been fired recently. He might have got off a shot before he died."

Logan shrugged. "Our guy might have been injured. We can check the nearby doctors and hospitals. I don't hold out much hope, though."

"If he or she was hurt badly enough that might explain why there haven't been any more murders," reasoned Jason.

"Except for the break-in at Dizzy's," Logan reminded them. "I doubt the incident wasn't connected to the murders. You know how I feel about the word *coincidence.*"

"So we're going on the theory that the killer wasn't injured or at least wasn't injured seriously," Zach said. "She or he checked out Dizzy's house but then has stayed quiet."

Too quiet. It was unnerving waiting for the murderer to make his move. Trying to anticipate what he might do or not do.

"Probably planning their next move," Logan replied. "When someone goes on a spree killing like this they aren't going to stop and go back to their regular life. They probably have a taste for–."

"Jesus, Mary, and Joseph," Jason swore, interrupting Logan. "Sorry about that but my assistant just handed me a message. Jenna Marshall was attacked in the parking garage at the mall this morning. She wasn't hurt badly, just some bruises and scrapes. She didn't get a good look at her attacker but she swears it was a woman. She could tell by the hands."

"Is our killer getting desperate?" Logan questioned, his brows pulled down. "This is the first time an attempt has failed."

"In broad daylight," Zach said in agreement. "It does have a whiff of desperation. Has she given a statement to the cops yet?"

"She was taken to the local emergency room where one of the patrolmen got her statement," Jason answered. "She was treated and then released. Leann and Dizzy want to go to Jenna's and visit, make sure she's okay, so I'm going to take them when I hang up with you. I'll email Jenna's statement to you. How about heading to the parking garage and checking it out? Maybe there are some security cameras this time. Then we can all meet at Jenna's. I know you'll want to talk to her personally but it might be a good idea to give her a little time to calm down. This had to be a nightmare for her. Thank god she fought her off."

Zach absolutely wanted to talk to Jenna. She probably remembered more than she gave herself credit for. In the meantime, he and Logan would visit the crime scene. If the killer was getting desperate, they might just be getting sloppy as well.

"We'll head there now," Zach replied, getting a nod in agreement from Logan. "I'll call you from the scene and let you know what we find."

All they needed was one good clue. Just one.

Chapter Twenty-Nine

JENNA HAD A few scrapes on her hands and knees, and a bruise on her cheek, but no major injuries. Leann made sure Jenna relaxed on the couch while Dizzy made tea for them all.

Leann's gaze swept the quiet home. "Are the children here? Do they know?"

Jenna accepted a cup of tea from Dizzy. "I sent them to stay with my parents for a few days. If someone is trying to kill me I don't want them anywhere near this."

"Of course," Leann said softly. "That's an excellent idea. Hopefully Zach and Jason will have the person responsible in custody soon."

Jenna's eyes flashed. "They're taking their time about it. In the meantime, people are dying. It was a woman who attacked me this morning and I bet it was that Nicole Quincy. They should go over there right now and arrest her."

Without any evidence? That would be unlikely.

"What would Nicole's motivation be?" Dizzy asked and Leann inwardly winced. Jenna had a bee in her bonnet when it came to Nicole.

"She's always been jealous of me," Jenna stated, slapping the delicate china cup into its saucer with a teeth-jarring clatter. "She's always wanted Drew but she couldn't have him. It's made her a bitter woman that wants revenge on people who are happy."

Dizzy's eyes widened and she gave Leann an alarmed glance. "I didn't realize that Nicole was that unhappy, but I don't know her that well."

"She could have killed me," Jenna insisted, her lips pressed into a flat line. "I was lucky I was able to run away and call for help, otherwise I would be dead. Then my children wouldn't have any parent at all."

"We're just glad you're okay," Leann replied, wanting to keep the conversation as calm as possible. She didn't want to add to Jenna's upset emotions. "Jason is going to double the guard on you."

A deputy had been doing the guarding duties but Jason had assigned one of his own men to assist. He was currently sitting in a dark SUV in front of the house after posting several cameras around the property.

Dizzy frowned. "How did the attacker get through the guard this morning?"

That was an excellent question.

"I told him that I didn't need a guard to go to the mall during the day. I asked him to drive the children to my parents' house so I knew they'd be safe."

The one time Jenna didn't have her guard she was attacked? The killer had to be watching. It also wasn't a smart move to go shopping by herself but Leann wasn't rude enough to point that out. She too wasn't thrilled about having a babysitter everywhere she went, but she put up with it because she wanted to stay alive.

The conversation waned as they sipped their tea. Dizzy had a strange look on her face and she was biting her lip. Leann wasn't sure what to say either. She didn't want to upset Jenna but she really wanted to ask some questions about what had happened in that parking garage.

"Is there anything we can do to give you a hand?" Dizzy asked, looking around. "Run some errands or do some grocery shopping?"

"That's sweet but I can't think of anything," Jenna replied with a grateful smile. "It's wonderful to have such good friends. Both of you have stuck by me through this awful time. But there is one thing I'd like to ask of you."

"Anything." Leann refilled Jenna's tea. "We're here for you."

"Will you hold my hand while I call my parents? They're going to be so upset and when they get upset, I'm going to get upset all over again."

Dizzy smiled and patted Jenna's hand. "Of course we will."

If the killer wanted them, they had to stick together.

✦ ✦ ✦

ZACH PACED THE perimeter of the area in the parking garage where Jenna was attacked and it didn't make any sense. In the aftermath, she must have been so upset and frightened that she'd scrambled her answers.

His partner Logan wasn't any happier, scowling and shaking his head. "This can't be right."

Rubbing his chin in thought, Zach couldn't argue. "She must have been dazed and confused afterward. That would explain her statement."

Logan pointed to the concrete floor. "She was standing about here when someone – a woman supposedly – came up behind her. Jenna said the woman wrapped an arm around her neck and pushed her to the floor. How tall is Jenna?"

"Five-five, maybe five-six."

"So the female attacker would have to be a few inches taller and pretty strong to take her straight down."

An image of the crime was being slowly constructed in Zach's brain. "But Jenna fought and got away."

"And ran that way according to her statement." Logan now pointed toward the next level of the parking garage. "That doesn't make any sense. Why didn't she run toward the street where there are people? She's parked on the first level and help wasn't that far away, yet she ran in the opposite direction. That doesn't make any sense."

That was the little detail that was bugging Zach as well.

"I'll play devil's advocate," he said, his gaze sweeping the open building. "Maybe the path to the street was blocked by her attacker so she had no choice but to run the other way. Perhaps she thought she could hide among the cars and get to the stairs or elevator."

"Okay, let's play that scene out. Come up behind me and then when I get away, block my path."

Wrapping his arm around Logan's throat, they lightly wrestled to the ground before Zach let go, letting Logan roll away. Zach stationed himself between Logan and the street as his friend jumped to his feet and turned to run.

Then Logan froze…staring right at Zach.

Logan pursed his lips. "If Jenna's attacker was in between her and safety, then Jenna had to have seen who it was but she says she didn't."

"So she definitely didn't run this way. Her statement has to be correct."

"So she ran in the opposite direction," Logan agreed. "But why? What was she thinking? Did she hear other people on that level?"

"Maybe she wasn't thinking at all and was in a panic? We can't expect untrained civilians to think like we do in a crisis situation. If she was in fight or flight mode, she probably just ran and to hell with the direction. She just wanted to get away."

"Maybe," Logan conceded. "It still doesn't make sense to me but you have a valid point. If she was terrified she might just run. But I can tell this is bothering you too. Spit it out."

Rubbing at his temples, Zach turned to face the street and then back to Logan. "How did she not see her attacker? You're right, if she tried to run this way she would have seen the woman. If she ran that way and the attacker pursued Jenna, is she then saying she never looked over her shoulder? She would have seen the attacker then. I would have looked over my shoulder."

Logan pulled out his phone and scrolled a few times. "Jenna says she ran that way and the attacker ran in the opposite direction. So if that's true, the attacker had to run down the street. There might be some cameras out there we can get some footage from."

"Where would she have parked?" Zach asked in frustration. "If she was waiting in the parking garage for Jenna, why didn't she park there too? Why attack Jenna and then have to make an escape on foot to wherever her car was stashed? None of this is logical. This killer was smart enough to murder more than once and get away with it. Now they attack Jenna unsuccessfully and have a lousy getaway plan. Is there something I'm missing here?"

Hands on his hips, Logan surveyed the crime scene. "There has to be more than what was in that statement. We're missing some key details."

"Agreed, and there's only one place to get those."

Chapter Thirty

JASON WAS SITTING in his truck in front of Jenna's house when Logan and Zach pulled up. There was also an unmarked police car in the driveway with a deputy in the driver's seat, trying to not look bored. Zach doubted the guards were allowed to read or play with their phone while they were on duty.

Rolling down the window when he saw them, Jason gave a mock salute. "I didn't expect to see you here. Is everything okay? How did the crime scene look?"

Zach rubbed at his chin and grimaced. "About that…it posed more questions than it answered. Her statement doesn't make any sense and isn't logical. We need to ask her more questions."

It was Jason's turn to wince. "Are you saying Jenna Marshall lied to the police? Shit, that's all we need today."

Chuckling, Logan leaned a hip against the side of the vehicle. "If she's telling the truth, she doesn't have a lick of sense. She ran in the opposite direction of help and people. Also, her statement that she didn't see her attacker doesn't hold water. I guess it's a possibility she didn't see who it was but hell, it's broad daylight and the garage was well lit."

"Maybe she has terrible eyesight," Jason suggested. "Maybe she's a nitwit. Crime happens to dumb people too."

"I need to see her answer my questions," Zach replied. "Watch her expressions and eyes. I think I'll be able to tell if she's lying. Even if I can't, one of us should be able to recognize a tell."

Blowing out a breath, Jason pushed open the truck door. "Why would she lie? For the attention?"

"It's as good a reason as any," Zach shrugged. "Maybe she liked the attention after Drew died and didn't want it to go away. Or maybe she's telling the truth and I'm off my game. Anything is possible."

"If she did it for the attention, you kind of have to feel sorry for her," Logan suggested as they approached the front door. "I mean, that's just sad, you know? She might be really lonely."

Zach extended his arm to ring the doorbell but paused, turning to Jason. "Is the deputy out here okay by himself?"

"He was by himself when we showed up, although they've got a cruiser coming by every fifteen minutes or so. Tonight they'll put a guard in the back as well, although if her story is bogus that won't be needed."

Zach wasn't sure what to believe at the moment. If Jenna had lied about being attacked it was clearly a cry for help and attention. After what she'd witnessed with her husband's death, she might want to talk to a professional. Someone who specialized in victims of crime. He hated to see anyone in so much pain they felt compelled to lie to the police.

The door swung open and Dizzy stood beckoning them to come in. "Come in. Jenna and Leann are in the kitchen making a grocery list. We finally convinced Jenna to let us go shopping and make some meals for her that she only has to heat up."

"How is she?" Zach asked. "The report said she only had some bumps and bruises."

He was particularly interested in what injuries she might have. If she'd falsified her statement to the cops, there still might be a good explanation for her wounds. Perhaps she'd used the story of an attacker to cover for someone else hurting her.

"She sort of alternates between anger and sadness," Dizzy replied, keeping her voice low. "She seems pretty calm right now."

Hopefully Jenna would stay that way once they started questioning her about this morning. Zach nudged Logan, holding him back before they entered the house.

"I'm going to watch her facial expressions and body language while you and Jason ask her questions."

Logan nodded. "Sounds good, especially as she already knows Jason and there should be some trust built already. I hope this turns out to be nothing."

So did Zach, but he had a bad feeling it was something. At the party Saturday night, Jenna had appeared to be a woman who liked attention but there had been no shortage of it. She wasn't someone who had to fake attacks to get people to see her. If anything, it was the opposite. She'd had friends and relatives in and out of the house all day, every day since Sunday.

Then there was the obvious logical path to follow.

If Jenna wasn't looking for attention, but she had indeed faked the attack…why? What did she gain from it? Was it to push the detectives to work faster, harder? Or was it to throw off the investigation? He feared it might be the latter. What was Jenna Marshall trying to hide?

Leann and Jenna were opening and closing cabinets in the kitchen, stopping every now and then to scribble items down on their list. Instead of the warm smile he'd come to expect from Leann whenever he saw her, she shifted her gaze to the piece of paper in front of her, not looking him in the eye.

Dammit.

This was all his fault and he needed to fix it. Now, however, wasn't exactly the moment. He'd talk to her later after they'd questioned Jenna. If he threw himself on Leann's mercy, surely she would forgive him? He'd acted like a prick this morning and he was sorry. She hadn't deserved how he'd treated her. Moving home and telling her family was a big deal and she needed to do it in her own time.

Dizzy had gathered up some of the cookies and a travel cup of coffee. "I'm going to take this snack out to the deputy. I'll be right back."

"Thank you," Jenna called out to the other woman's retreating figure. "Good afternoon, gentlemen. I didn't expect you."

"Sorry to drop in unannounced," Jason apologized. "But we really need to speak with you about what happened this morning. Would you mind answering a few more questions? I know you gave your statement to the police but we're just here to clarify a few points."

Zach placed his hand on Logan's shoulder. "I'm not sure if you've met Jason's partner Logan Wright. Logan, this is Jenna Marshall."

"Ma'am, it's a pleasure to meet you."

Logan had a way with the ladies without even trying. Maybe it was the man's smile or his tone of voice but women seemed to love it and him.

"Can we get you something to drink?" Leann asked, studiously avoiding Zach's gaze as she opened the refrigerator to inspect its contents. Instead of looking at him she was checking the date on the milk.

"We're good," her brother replied, turning his attention back to Jenna. "So can you tell us again how the attacker came at you? I think you said it was from behind."

Jenna's cheeks burned red. "I'm not sure I want to talk about this again. It's very upsetting."

"I know it is, ma'am," Logan said. "But it would help us with our investigation. Just a few questions?"

Chewing on her lip, Jenna nodded. "Fine, just a couple. Yes, she came at me from behind. Grabbed me around the neck and wrestled me to the ground." Her fingers came up to touch the bruise on her cheek. "My head hit the concrete and that's where I got this."

"What made you decide it was a woman?" Jason asked.

"Her hands were definitely female." Jenna huffed out a breath. "I don't know why we're talking about this. I told the officer that the woman who attacked me was Nicole Quincy. You should be at her house asking her questions, not me."

This was the first Zach was hearing about Nicole Quincy. "Why do you think it was Nicole? Did you get a look at her?"

Jenna shook her head. "No, but I know it was her. She's been jealous of me for years. I think she killed Drew because she couldn't have him."

"What about the other victims?" Logan queried. "Why did she kill them?"

"Decoys," Jenna replied. "She killed them to throw off the investigation."

That was a very interesting theory and it could be true, but Zach doubted that Nicole Quincy had thought it up. Jenna's body language was closed, with her arms crossed over her chest and her hand lifted to cover her throat in a protective gesture. She wasn't making eye contact either.

Zach's gut was screaming that Jenna was hiding something and there was a hell of a lot more to this story than getting jumped in a parking garage.

Logan cleared his throat to continue. "Jenna, I want to be sure that we have the details of the attack correct. You said that you ran toward the next level in the parking garage to get away from your attacker. Is that correct?"

"It is."

"Why didn't you run toward the street? Toward the people?"

Jenna threw up her hands. "I couldn't. She was in my way."

"So you tried to run that way but she blocked your path?"

"Exactly," Jenna smiled. "That's exactly what happened."

Logan had her right where he wanted her. "Then how did you not see her face? You turned to run toward the street but she was blocking your path. She would have been right in front of you."

"No," Jenna sputtered, clearly shaken by Logan's observation. "That's not how it happened. You're twisting my words."

"Then how did you know she was in your path?" Jason asked softly.

"That's where she was standing." Jenna's voice rose and her body was visibly shaking. She didn't like being put on the spot. Not one bit. "Between me and the road. I couldn't go that way."

"You said you were facing east," Logan reminded her. "That meant the road was on your left and she was behind you, so she couldn't have been blocking you."

Caught in a lie, Jenna wasn't going to go down without a fight. Zach watched as her chin lifted with determination.

"No, you're not listening." Jenna shook her head again. "I didn't see her but she was blocking the path. I had to run up and I went to the elevators."

"Did you push the button for the elevators?" Zach asked and then cursed his loose tongue. It was his own idea to let the others do the questioning but his senses were on high alert. Jenna was slapping lie upon lie and he wanted to know why. She was clearly hiding something and he had a terrible, awful feeling what it was.

The other victims might have been decoys but it wasn't because Nicole Quincy had wanted Drew dead. It was because Jenna wanted her husband dead. It was one of the oldest stories in the book – one spouse murdering another.

"They don't come any other way," Jenna replied acidly. "That's how elevators work."

All they needed to do was keep putting on the pressure. Jenna hadn't expected to be pressed on her story and she wasn't prepared. She'd assumed she'd be treated as the grieving widow and a victim.

"How long did it take for the elevator doors to open?"

"I don't know. A few seconds maybe? Is it important? I got

away and I'm still alive."

Patience. Just be patient.

"You're sure the elevator doors opened? Did you get in the elevator?"

She'd taken a step back, an instinctive move to get away from Zach but he wasn't going anywhere. "I took it to the third floor, got out, and headed into the mall where I flagged down a security guard. But you already know all of that."

"Actually, this part wasn't in your statement. You told the officer that you ran into the mall to get help from a security guard. There was no mention of you taking the elevator to do it."

She shrugged carelessly. "I just remembered."

Now. The time is right…now.

"Do you remember the Out of Order sign on the elevators? Because when I went to check out the crime scene today the elevators weren't working."

Her mouth fell open and her eyes widened comically. She seemed to be having trouble replying. "I–I mean–It wasn't broken this morning."

Jenna's face had gone ashen and she leaned back against the kitchen counter. Leann's attention had been on her grocery list but it was now firmly on her friend from high school, her expression horrified as she realized Jenna was lying through her teeth. A smart woman, Leann had to be putting this together in her own mind and coming up with a pretty suspicious theory of what was going on.

"So it broke sometime after your attack and when Logan and I arrived?" Zach said. "I guess I can check with maintenance.

They're the ones that put that sign there."

Jenna nodded vigorously. "You do that. They'll tell you."

Why not go for broke?

"I also received a call from our computer expert. He pulled the traffic camera from the light in front of the parking garage and there was no one running from the scene at the time of your attack. Are you sure she ran toward the sidewalk?"

Jenna's hand had flown up to her throat again. "I'm sure. Completely sure. Maybe she ducked out of the way. Criminals know how to do that, right?"

"Some do," he conceded. "Some don't. As a rule most criminals are quite stupid. They all eventually get caught because they do something dumb. They get careless and cocky."

Jenna was trembling and her face had gone a horrible ghostly white. "I don't want to answer any more questions. You all need to leave."

Zach took a few steps closer to her, but slowly, as he didn't want to spook her. He needed to get between her and Leann, especially with a butcher block full of knives sitting on the counter. Jenna might give in peacefully or she might fight. If it was the latter, Zach didn't want to give her any ammunition. "I think we both know that I can't do that, Jenna."

Lips trembling, a few tears streaked down her pale cheeks. Realization had dawned in her eyes that he knew what she'd been trying to hide. There was no more reason to lie.

"You don't understand."

Now they were getting somewhere.

With one eye on Jenna, Zach ever so slowly sidled closer to her, insinuating himself between her and Leann. Everyone else was far enough away that he didn't have to worry about them.

"Help me understand, Jenna. Tell me why."

✦ ✦ ✦

ZACH'S HAND WAS firmly in the small of Leann's back, pushing her away from Jenna and toward Jason and Dizzy. Her brother reached for her as she moved closer, tugging her to his side with Dizzy on his other arm.

"Are you okay?" Jason whispered.

Leann nodded, still shocked by what appeared to be unwinding in front of them. Jenna was acting strange, stranger even than earlier, and from the expression on Zach's face there was much more going on than simply asking her about the attack this morning.

"You weren't accosted this morning," Zach stated. In no way did he make it sound like a question.

"No," Jenna said softly, her gaze seeming to go somewhere far away. She wasn't looking at Zach or any of them; instead her eyes were focused off into the distance.

"Why did you pretend?"

"To blame Nicole."

Jenna's hands were wrung together, the knuckles white. More tears were falling and it was then that Leann put the puzzle together.

Jenna had done all of this. She'd killed those people. But why? Why on earth would she do something so horrifying?

It was only when Jenna and Zach's heads turned toward her that Leann realized she's spoken her question aloud.

Jenna's face turned red and angry. "Drew cheated on me. He

got Carole pregnant. But then you knew that, didn't you? You all knew. All my supposed loyal friends but you kept this from me. A real friend would have told me. I deserved to know."

Leann wasn't sure what her friend was talking about. Drew had gone out with Carole once in their junior year but had he done it again recently? And what was this about a baby?

"Carole was pregnant?" Leann asked, frowning, searching her memories of high school. "When did this happen? I truly don't know what you're talking about, Jenna."

Crossing her arms over her chest, Jenna took a step forward but Zach didn't let her get any closer. "You know all of this. You all knew. Drew got Carole pregnant and her parents sent her away to have the baby. That's why she was late starting senior year."

Shock rippled through Leann as she processed Jenna's words. She remembered that Carole had been late coming to school that year and she hadn't been able to run for senior class president, but she'd had no idea that Carole had been pregnant. And with Drew's baby.

"That's why you killed Drew," Zach said. "You were angry that he'd never told you."

Silvery tears streamed down Jenna's cheeks and she slid down to the floor, her back against the cabinets. Zach knelt down next to her, patting her on the hand.

"He should have told me. Everyone should have told me."

"Is that why you killed the others?" Zach asked, glancing over his shoulder at Leann. "You wanted your revenge on them because they kept it a secret?"

Jenna scrubbed at her wet face and nodded. "When I found

out I hated Drew and everyone else. They deserved to die for what they did to me. Leann was next but I couldn't get to her."

Leann hadn't known, though. Had the others or was this just a fantasy inside of Jenna's head?

Zach stood and then helped Jenna to her feet. "I have to take you in, Jenna. You know that, right? Is there anyone you want me to call for you? Your family? A lawyer?"

The bouncy, cute blonde that Jenna had been was gone and in her place was a shattered woman who looked far older than her actual age. Grey skin, red-rimmed eyes, a broken expression. Jenna was swaying on her feet and crying, rocking back and forth as if to self-soothe.

"There's no one. Everyone I thought cared about me is gone."

Jason was on the phone to the chief of police and Zach had led Jenna to the kitchen table so she could sit down. There were so many questions still unanswered. How had a beautiful wife and mother of two snapped and killed four people? Drew was dead and Jenna was going away for a long time, maybe forever. Those children had lost both their parents.

All because of something that had happened fifteen years ago when they were just dumb teenagers.

Chapter Thirty-One

LEANN WAS PACKING up her belongings in Zach's home when she heard the front door open and the sound of boots on the stairs. Shit, she'd hoped to be gone by the time he returned. She didn't want any messy scenes. He'd walked away this morning because she'd been too lily-livered to tell her family she was staying so she didn't want to assume that he even wanted her here. Making herself scarce seemed like the best option.

"You're leaving."

Yes, but I don't want to.

Tucking a blouse into the suitcase, she turned to face Zach who was standing in the doorway. Leann searched his expression for some sort of clue as to what he was thinking or feeling but he was wearing his best poker face. Completely expressionless. He could have won the lottery or been fired from his job for all he was giving away.

"You caught the killer," she reminded him, her voice shaky with emotion. "I'm not in danger anymore. Did Jenna tell you more when you took her to the station?"

Hopefully he would think she was agitated because of Jenna and not because of their falling out this morning.

"She did. Once she realized that we had her I guess she didn't see much point in keeping quiet. Honestly, it seemed like she wanted to tell someone so that they would be on her side. If she hadn't killed anyone I met have felt sorry for her." Zach entered the bedroom and leaned up against the dresser. "She'd convinced Darrell to help her by pretending to be in love with him. She was the blonde he was meeting at the hotel. From what I can guess, she was using sex to control him. He killed Bitty and Drew but she killed Carole. Eventually she had to get rid of him too. The plan was to pin the murders on Nicole Quincy. She battered her own face against a car this morning to get that bruise."

She wasn't sure she wanted to know but… "And me?"

Zach lips flattened into a line. "You were the last on the list but she couldn't get to you. When she broke into Dizzy's she realized you weren't staying there so she'd planned to be patient, waiting until we dropped our guard. She said she was hoping to make it look like an accident, although she wasn't sure how."

"I didn't even know about the baby. I wasn't keeping anything from her."

"We don't even know if there really was a baby," Zach shrugged. "She only found out because Drew got drunk one night, they argued, and he told her. He could have been goading her or he could have been telling the truth. From what Jenna says, they'd talked divorce a few times. Drew had several extramarital affairs and she was tired of it. But apparently, the baby thing was more than she could handle. When she found out, that's when she started planning her revenge."

Exhaling slowly, Leann sat down on the bed, a folded sweater on her lap. "And now she'll go to prison."

"I kind of got the feeling she always knew she would," Zach replied. "She didn't seem shocked and she hasn't lawyered up. She's completely cooperated with us and answered every question we've asked. I think she's relieved in a way. She's been a deeply unhappy woman for a long time."

Leann placed the sweater on top of the neat pile of clothes in the suitcase. "I didn't see it at all. I've known Jenna since we were kids but I didn't see that she was a cold-blooded killer."

"Don't blame yourself. No one saw this."

Rubbing at her aching temples, she tried to laugh. "You did."

"Not until it was staring me in the face and after I had eliminated pretty much every other variable. I didn't want it to be her."

"All because she thought we'd kept a secret from her. Do you think she has an insanity defense?"

Killing four people wasn't the hallmark of good mental health.

"That's not for me to say but she appears to grasp that what she's done is wrong, and she just doesn't have much – if any – remorse for her actions. She feels she was justified and that they deserved what they got."

"You saved my life. My best friend from childhood was planning to murder me."

It was a reality that Leann still hadn't quite grasped. She was hoping she might simply wake up and find all of this had been a bad dream.

"Nothing and no one was going to get near you."

Leann's heart ached in her chest, hearing the force behind Zach's words. She believed him because that's who he was. No matter how he might feel about her, he'd do his job.

She busied her hands folding a pair of jeans. "You should have been born an Anderson male. You're so much like my father and brothers. I mean that as a compliment."

"I took it as one."

The silence was awkward as she moved the clothes around in her suitcase and she studiously avoided his gaze that saw way too much. She couldn't allow him to see how much she was hurting. Walking away from him today was more painful than she'd ever imagined, and she only had herself to blame.

"I'll never understand why it's hard to pack to go home but easy to pack to leave on a trip. It's like the clothes expand or something. Everything easily fit when I came here."

Now she was stupidly rambling in a desperate attempt to act like everything was totally normal. The sooner she got out of this house the better off she'd be. If she stayed much longer he was going to see how upset she was.

She'd been trying to stuff a pair of high heels into her suitcase but his large hands came down over hers, halting her progress.

"Leann, what are you doing?"

She couldn't look at him. Despite the thick tension between them, his tone had been gentle and soft.

"Packing. What does it look like I'm doing?"

Her throat tightened painfully as his fingers closed over hers, strong and warm.

"It looks like you're running away."

Which was exactly what she was doing but they both knew why.

"It's time to go."

The words came out choked and she had to clear her throat several times to be able to speak clearly.

"Are you going to stay at Dizzy's?"

Leann nodded and tugged her hands from Zach's hold. "She's waiting for me."

"Can she wait a few minutes more?"

He wanted to prolong this agony? Was he some sort of sadist?

"Wait for what?"

There was a long sigh and then a grunt as Zach lifted the suitcase up and tossed it onto a chair. "Dammit, woman, we need to talk. Look at me, Leann."

No. If I do I might cry.

"Zach..."

This time it was her he lifted up, but instead of throwing her on the bed he set her down gently next to him on the mattress. "Leann, we had a fight this morning. People argue. It's going to happen. It doesn't mean you run and we never work it out. Unless that's what you want. Do you want to end things?"

The answer flew out of her mouth before she could stop it. "No, I don't."

His fingers gently lifted her chin so she was looking up into his tender blue gaze. "Good. Neither do I. We had a fight, honey, but that doesn't mean we can't talk about it. For my part, I'm sorry. I shouldn't have pushed you. When you're ready, you're ready and not a moment before."

"It wasn't your fault." Leann shook her head, determined to take responsibility for the debacle that was this morning. "It was all me. It's my issue with my family, and I wasn't acting like the adult that I keep telling them that I am. But…I told Jason today and I'm going to tell my parents at dinner tomorrow night. I don't know why I hesitated this morning. The whole incident was stupid and I wanted to take back those words the minute I said them. I'm so sorry, Zach."

"We're both sorry and neither one of us acted too mature." Zach smiled, showing off that dimple in his cheek. "Honey, I'm going to get mad every now and then. You are too. Let's not throw out what's good because of a few bad moments."

Her eyes teared up and a few slipped down her cheeks. "I thought I had pushed you away."

Pulling her into his lap, Zach growled, low and sexy, burying his face into the crook of her neck. "You're going to have to try a hell of a lot harder than that to get rid of me. If you'd left today before I got home I would have just followed you. We've got something here that's special, Leann." He lifted his head, his fingertips grazing her lips. "I was going to tell you last night but I got scared. I think…I love you. No, I know I do. Shit, I know it hasn't been very long and I don't expect you to say it back or anything–"

"I love you," she interrupted his rambling, happy in the knowledge that he was just as nervous as she was. "I love you, too."

His lips devoured hers, tasting, testing, and then claiming. At some point she'd climbed onto his lap, straddling his thighs, her fingers clinging tightly to his wide shoulders. When he finally lifted his head, she could see the joy inside of her clearly reflected in his own expression. She hadn't ruined everything after all. They had a chance, a future.

"You could come back to Florida with me," she suggested. "Help me pack and put my condo on the market. That way I could get here faster. I'll even take you to Disney World."

"I might take you up on that offer. If my employer will give me some time off, that is."

Leann has a feeling that her brother Jason would be so grateful that she was moving home that he'd give Zach all the time off he wanted.

"I think that could be arranged. It's funny, I wasn't sure coming home for this reunion was the right thing to do. But if I hadn't then we wouldn't be together."

Chuckling, Zach waggled his brows. "Honey, the first time I saw you I was knocked out by your smile. I have a feeling that this might have happened no matter what. It simply would have taken a little more time."

Remembering the first time she'd met Zach she couldn't disagree, although her brothers were going to try and take credit for all of this. They'd be even more insufferable than they usually were. She was so incredibly happy she just might let them think that they were responsible.

"Kiss me again? I can't believe this is really happening."

His lips pressed against hers and a million butterflies flew free in her abdomen. This was the feeling she'd been waiting and hoping for. Leann had come full circle, returning to Tremont only to find what she'd been out seeking elsewhere. Family, friends, happiness, and love. It was unexpected but not unwelcome.

Leann was in love. And when an Anderson fell…it was forever. She couldn't wait to move back and start her new life with her new love. But first she needed one more kiss…

Chapter Thirty-Two

Six months later…

ZACH LIT THE last candle and stepped back to survey the effect. He'd made a special dinner for Leann and he wanted tonight to be as romantic as possible. He had an important question to ask her.

The meal was prepared and keeping warm in the kitchen. The dining room table was set with a snowy white tablecloth, a centerpiece of roses, and Leann's mother's best silver and china. When he'd talked to David and Elaine, she'd insisted Zach use them.

For good luck, she'd said. He hoped he didn't need it but he wasn't going to take any chances.

Sweating nervously through his shirt, he flew up the stairs and ripped it off, quickly tugging on a fresh white button down and tucking it into his pants. Leann would be home any minute and she had no idea he was even back in Tremont. She thought he was still in Denver working on a case. Though she was officially living with Dizzy at the moment, she stayed at his place when he was out of town to water the plants and generally keep an eye on things.

The sound of her key in the front door had him flying back down the stairs so he was standing there waiting for her when she walked in. Looking beautiful but tired, her eyes widened when she realized he was there and she tossed her briefcase away to run into his open arms.

"Why didn't you call and tell me you were home?" she scolded him, placing kisses on his lips, cheeks, chin, and nose. "I would have picked you up at the airport."

Taking his time, he pressed his lips to hers, drinking in the sweetness that was purely Leann. She tasted of coffee and chocolate and love. They were both breathless when he finally broke the kiss.

"I wanted to surprise you. Besides, I know you had a full day of meetings now that you're a big important businesswoman at Anderson Industries."

Leann had taken over as the head of all Human Resource functions under the Anderson business umbrella. Even her cousin Easton, who was notoriously quiet, raved about how she was updating their operation.

Rolling her eyes, she shrugged off her navy blue jacket and kicked off her high heels. "I'm going to ignore that as nothing about this job is glamorous. I was actually on a ladder today digging through old employee files that are going to go electronic."

"Then I'll pour you a glass of wine and let you relax while I serve dinner." He dropped a kiss on her cheek. "I love you, baby."

"Love you too."

He'd calmed down for a few minutes when Leann walked in but now his heart was racing again, battering his ribs. He was fucking nervous. He couldn't remember the last time he'd been this shaken. He'd stared down a murderer last week and he hadn't been this scared.

What if she said no?

Slinking into the kitchen, he popped open the champagne and poured two glasses of the golden liquid before carrying returning to Leann. She was standing by the dining room table staring at the romantic setting he'd created, a smile curving her lips.

"You certainly have surprised me, you handsome devil. Someone is in a romantic mood tonight."

Handing her the glass, he held up his own champagne. "How about a toast? To us. It just gets better and better."

Clinking glasses, she smiled and sipped her drink. "I'll definitely drink to that because it's so true. We do get better at this relationship stuff every day."

Passing a hand over the back of his damp neck, he nodded toward the table. "Why don't you sit down and I'll bring dinner out? I hope you're hungry."

The next half-hour or so were almost normal. They ate and chatted about his business trip and her projects at work. She complimented the chicken and he promised to teach her how to make it. They sipped at the champagne while his blood pressure continued to steadily rise until he thought his head was going to explode off of his body, spin around, and come to rest in the middle of the table like some sort of macabre centerpiece.

Zach wanted to do it at just the right moment but that moment hadn't arrived yet. Maybe he should somehow create the opening…

"You know, I missed you when I was away," he began. "I'm becoming used to sleeping next to you."

She wrinkled her nose and groaned. "I know I snore. You're a saint to put up with it."

What the hell? What was he waiting for?

Do it, man. Take the chance.

Chuckling, he reached for her hand, tangling the fingers with his own. "It would be my privilege to listen to you snore every night for the rest of my life."

Leann laughed and shook her head. "You are romantic tonight. Luckily for you, you don't have to do that."

She wasn't getting where he was going with this.

"What if I want to?"

She opened her mouth to answer but no words came. Blinking, she seemed to think about what he'd said. "Why…I mean…why would you want to do that?"

"Because I love you, Leann."

She licked her lips and for once he was happy to see that she was as nervous as he was.

"Every night is a long time," she said, her voice cracking at the end. "A long, long time."

He'd been rehearsing this part all day. Hopefully he wouldn't fuck it up.

"Forever wouldn't be long enough." Sliding out of his chair, he knelt on bended knee in front of her. Her hand flew to her lips and she gasped, the color high in her cheeks. He'd surprised her for sure. She hadn't been expecting this. "I love you, Leann

Anderson. And I want to spend the rest of my life with you. The good days and the bad. In sickness and in health and all the other vows that there are. Will you marry me, baby? You'd make me the happiest man on earth if you'd say yes."

More sweating. More pounding in his chest. He was actually a little lightheaded and dizzy. She wasn't saying anything, looking totally stunned.

"Baby?" he prompted. They both couldn't faint. One of them had to stay conscious.

She let out a long breath and made a squeaking sound that he couldn't identify. He wasn't breathing all that well either. He reminded himself to exhale.

"Was that a yes or a no or a maybe?"

"Yes!" she gasped, falling to the floor with him, her arms wrapping around his body and hugging and kissing him for all she was worth. "Yes, of course I'll marry you. I love you."

Cupping her face in his hands, he leaned down to give her a slow kiss as his heart sped up even faster than before like it might take flight out of his chest. She'd said yes.

Yes.

She was going to be his wife and he was going to be her husband. They were going to build a life together.

Just as soon as he remembered how to walk and talk because they were still on the hardwood floor, sprawled together in a tangle of arms and legs as they kissed and held each other, oblivious to their surroundings. Neither one wanted to break the spell cast over them. They were getting married.

He found his tongue and managed a few words. "I'm going to be the best husband I can be, honey. I swear it."

Her fingers traced the line of his jaw and she looked up at him with such love in her gaze that his chest physically hurt. He couldn't imagine what he'd done to deserve this woman but he'd make sure she was happy every day of her life.

"I know you will be. But remember what you told me…we're still going to fight and get mad. The secret is not to stay that way."

At this moment, Zach couldn't imagine being angry with this amazing woman who had just agreed to be his wife. Of course, that feeling of euphoria wouldn't last forever. They'd fuss at each other and disagree about the thermostat and what movie to watch. But with Leann he had found the one thing he'd always dreamed of. They'd build it together one brick at time. A home full of love and laughter.

I hope you enjoyed Zach and Leann's happily ever after! Look for Dizzy's story in Window To Danger coming soon!

Thank you for reading Reunited With Danger!

Don't miss a thing!
Sign up to be notified of Olivia's new releases:

oliviajaymesoptin.instapage.com

About The Author

Olivia Jaymes is a wife, mother, lover of sexy romance, and caffeine addict. She lives with her husband and son in central Florida and spends her days with handsome alpha males and spunky heroines.

She is currently working on a new contemporary romance series – The Hollywood Showmance Chronicles in addition to the ongoing Danger Incorporated series.

Visit Olivia Jaymes at

www.OliviaJaymes.com

Danger Incorporated

Damsel In Danger

Hiding From Danger

Discarded Heart Novella

Indecent Danger

Embracing Danger

Danger In The Night

Reunited With Danger

Cowboy Justice Association

Cowboy Command

Justice Healed

Cowboy Truth

Cowboy Famous

Cowboy Cool

Imperfect Justice

The Deputies

Justice Inked

Justice Reborn

Military Moguls

Champagne and Bullets

Diamonds and Revolvers

Caviar and Covert Ops

Emeralds, Rubies, and Camouflage

www.ingramcontent.com/pod-product-compliance
Lightning Source LLC
Chambersburg PA
CBHW020308200626
46814CB00006BA/2143

* 9 7 8 1 9 4 4 4 9 0 2 5 6 *